Ballet Academy

Dance Steps

BEATRICE MASINI

Translation by Laura Watkinson

PICCADILLY PRESS • LONDON

First published in Great Britain in 2009
by Piccadilly Press Ltd,
5 Castle Road, London NW1 8PR
www.piccadillypress.co.uk

Text copyright © Beatrice Masini, 2005

Translated from the original *A Passo di Danza*,
published by Edizioni EL, Trieste, Italy
www.edizioniel.com
Published by arrangement with Rights People, London

A catalogue record for this book is available
from the British Library

ISBN: 978 1 84812 022 8

Printed in the UK by CPI Bookmarque, Croydon, CR0 4TD
Cover design by Patrick Knowles
Cover illustration by Sara Not

Ballet Academy

CHAPTER ONE

A Day Like Any Other

'And one, and two, and three, and four. And one, and two, and three, and four. Anna, pay attention to your wrist. Francine, your shoulders. And three, and four . . .'

Zoe hated doing *pliés*. She'd always hated them, ever since she was a little girl of five. She'd never understood the point of all that bending low with your knees going out, while you kept your back very straight. Then there was the problem that when she was doing *pliés*, her feet had the annoying tendency to turn inwards and flop in a weak and feeble way – exactly how they shouldn't be.

'Zoe, straighten your feet. Nice and flat. *Flat.* Do you understand?'

Yes, Zoe understood. As flat as a pancake. As flat as a flatfish flattened on a flat floor. Zoe imagined a long line of fish, dead ones, arranged at regular intervals, in three rows, their eyes dim. Their teacher, Madame Olenska, would be happy then, wouldn't she? You couldn't get much flatter than that.

She suddenly felt like laughing, but managed to smother her giggles with a cough. Madame Olenska glared at her anyway. One mustn't cough, one mustn't sneeze, one mustn't scratch, and one mustn't laugh. *May we please breathe, Madame?* Zoe thought. Some days she was sure the answer would be no.

Zoe laughed to herself, but very quietly, just gently through her nose. And she carried on going up and down, up and down, a little elevator controlled by the music and by Madame Olenska's commands. After a while, she stopped thinking about it, and then she became aware that she wasn't thinking about it, and realised that, in fact, that was the way movement should be. Her body clearly could do what it was supposed to – obey her and and behave itself properly (well, most of the time, anyway), so why was her mind so rebellious?

It was probably a question of personality. Zoe took advantage of a swift *renversée* to glance in the mirror at the empty, perfect doll's face that belonged to Laila. Laila was French. Laila never rebelled. She didn't laugh, didn't fidget, didn't talk in class. Everything that she did was perfect and it seemed effortless for her – as if she didn't have to think about it at all.

Despite this, Zoe knew she would never want to trade places with her, even if Laila *was* the best in the class, and therefore Madame Olenska's favourite. To Zoe, she looked just like one of those dolls with a key in their backs – the clockwork sort that you wind up and which then always move in the same way, with the same sequence of gestures, always following someone else's instructions. Zoe was happier being a *real* girl – one who made mistakes and got into muddles – even if that meant she wasn't perfect. At the Academy, *perfection* was a word that seemed to be carved in letters of gold and diamonds above all the doors, a word that sparkled and demanded that every student should sparkle too.

Madame Olenska clapped her hands together sharply, breaking Zoe's thoughts.

'The lesson is over. You may leave. *Au revoir*,' she said, as she did every day.

They responded in a singsong chorus, '*Au revoir*, Madame.'

Zoe wasn't very good at pronouncing the soft French 'r', even though she'd tried a thousand times to say it properly, standing at home in front of the mirror. Naturally, the words slipped from Laila's mouth as sweet as honey, but then, of course, she was French. Never mind, once they were through the classroom door, she could shrug her shoulders and even pull faces behind Laila's back. No one was going to tell tales on her, because no one else liked Laila either.

Somebody slipped an arm through Zoe's. It was Leda.

'Are you still mad at her?' Leda whispered, nodding towards Laila. She fell into step beside her best friend. It wasn't an easy task. Leda had grown so tall recently – she'd suddenly shot up and already looked like a teenager, while Zoe still had the size and proportions of a little girl. It was strange because they'd been the same size for so many years. Zoe was glad it was the only thing that had ever changed between the two of them.

'No, I'm not mad at her,' replied Zoe, almost reluctantly. 'I'm mad at *myself* for being mad at her. I mean, it's stupid. She's just Laila and she can't help seeming prim and superior. It's not her fault – she's just like that.'

'Hmm, maybe she doesn't even realise how she's behaving, or maybe she doesn't like the way she is, but doesn't know how to change. After all, we don't really know her very well, do we?' said Leda, sympathetically.

That was typical Leda – she really did have a kind heart. She wasn't just good in a dull kind of way, she was always thoughtful and she paid attention to other people and their feelings. It was just one of the reasons Zoe liked her so much.

They stopped talking, because you weren't allowed to talk in the corridors. You couldn't run in the corridors at the Academy either. But once they reached the changing rooms it was a different matter – the class suddenly transformed. With a frenzy of freedom from classes, they pushed and crowded together, ran and jostled to the benches where their clothes were waiting in varying degrees of disorder, stuffed into big bags hanging from the clothes hooks. No one cared if tights were put on inside out, if T-shirts fell below jumpers. Perfection was no longer a sacred word and normality took over.

With everyone feeling relieved that another rule-filled day was over, it was finally time to go home.

When she slipped under the side portico of the Ballet Academy and walked through the artists' entrance each morning, Zoe always felt very proud, even though she'd been doing it for five years.

Leaving the building in the afternoon was a different matter. She always felt very slightly relieved. She was heading back to normal life: to friends, family and fun. Zoe said goodbye to Leda and walked to the bus stop. She had only been allowed to travel on her own this year, after much pestering of her parents, and it still excited her. The bus pulled up and Zoe got on, letting the hardships of the day melt away as she thought about the evening ahead.

As always, Zoe rang the doorbell, just once. Her mum opened the door and gave her a hug. Then she had a snack and settled down to watch television for a while. Her mum joined her on the sofa, as she always did when she had the time.

They watched one of those programmes with witches or fairies in, which always seemed more or less the same. As Zoe watched the whirl of colours, magic potions and spells, almost without realising, she gradually started to lean on her mum, until her entire body was slumped against her, like a sloth, soft with sleepiness and keen for cuddles. And then, just at that moment . . .

'Mummy, why do you only love Zoe?'

For some months now, that had been Maria's favourite question and Zoe never knew whether to smile or to feel a little worried. Of course, Maria was only little but you had to try to understand her point of view. Zoe had been trying to understand her for six years now without much success. As usual, Maria's question was followed by a thud on the sofa, and then a tiny but insistent presence squeezed its way into the cosy cuddle Zoe was having with her mum. Maria wriggled in between them like a stubborn little caterpillar, twisting around to separate them. Was she really jealous? Or was it just a game, a little ritual of hers?

'You know I love all three of you the same,' Mum said, like someone repeating a refrain without even thinking about the words. 'You *do* know that, don't you?'

'Yes, but I want to watch television with you too.'

The duo became a trio, and slowly Zoe settled back down to watch the programme again. Maria was noisy though, and sang along with all the theme songs.

A bit later, Zoe felt a shadow over her. 'Oh, look at that, the gang's all here.'

'Come on, Sara, come and join us,' Mum said.

Zoe's older sister Sara flopped on to the sofa with a small sigh and Maria climbed on to her. Just for a while, they all sat together.

At one time, Zoe and her sister Sara were good friends. After all, there were only three years between them and they shared the same room and the same toys. Sara even used to dress Zoe up and put make-up on her and pretend she was a living doll and then show her off to her friends, who were a bit jealous because they only had brothers, the poor things. Then everything changed. Zoe started going to Ballet Academy, and Maria was born. They moved to a new house and everyone had their own bedroom. Zoe and Sara grew apart. Sara was grown-up now – she wore real make-up, even though she wasn't supposed to. Heaven help anyone who told on her though. But Zoe wouldn't dream of doing that – Maria was the one with the big mouth.

Now Zoe and Sara were more like two classmates who had been put next to each other. They had nothing in common and no desire to find out if they had anything in common. But as they sat together on the sofa, Zoe wondered if they might grow close again.

The programme finished and Mum switched off the television.

'I have to go and play now,' announced Maria, and she slid off the sofa to go to her room.

Sara got up and left too, without saying anything. In another few minutes, Mum left too, and Zoe knew the cosy time was over for another day.

Zoe was always the one who helped to lay the table in the evening. One of the advantages of Ballet Academy was that there was no homework to do during the week. Dad was at home all day on Saturday and Sunday, and on those days he took care of the evening meal from start to finish, from shopping and cooking to laying the table. His *pasta al forno* was the best in the world.

However, as it was a Thursday evening, it was Zoe who picked the colour of the paper napkins, so that they matched the tablecloth, and took care of everything else as well. As she set the table, she chatted with her mum.

'How's Leda?' her mum asked her, pouring herself a glass of white wine. 'You haven't invited her over for a while.'

'I have invited her,' said Zoe, 'but she always says no. I think she feels self-conscious now she has grown so tall.'

'Oh dear. But she needn't worry – no one's going to stare at her here. Leda . . . it's a good name for a ballerina.'

'Why?'

'Well, did you know that her name comes from a Greek myth? Leda was a beautiful girl and Zeus, the king of the gods, fell in love with her. To win her over, he transformed himself into a swan.'

'All ballerinas are a bit like swans, aren't they?' Zoe replied.

She had a clear memory from when she was little – only three years old – when she went to see a ballet for the first time with her family. It wasn't *Swan Lake*, it was *Giselle*, but the ballerinas with their long white tutus and their soft, agile arms had looked like swans gliding over a lake.

'Oh, absolutely,' said her mum. 'But maybe she feels a little more like the ugly duckling at the moment.'

'She's better off than Anna, though. At least she's still got nice, smooth skin. Well, normal skin, anyway. Anna's covered in spots, poor thing. And she hasn't eaten any chocolate for months.'

'They'll pass soon enough,' said Zoe's mum. 'It's all part of growing up.' She smiled. 'When you were all little, there weren't any of these sorts of problems.'

'No, that's true,' said Zoe. 'We just had to be good little girls.'

'And you all were good little girls, back then. You were good and sweet and full of life and all you wanted was to become even better. Oh, my goodness! The water's boiling.'

Her mum got up and went to check the pasta. Zoe slipped out of the kitchen. She stopped in front of the long mirror in the hall and felt happy about what she saw. The girl looking back at her was not too tall, nor too short, not fat and not too thin. She had long legs – you could see that even when she was wearing jeans. And the wrists emerging from the sleeves of her jumper were slender ones. Her hair was still in the tight bun the school insisted on, but some strands had slipped out of the hair-pins and were softening the contours of her face, which was longish, with sharp cheekbones. She had big, hazel eyes – honey eyes, her dad said – pale eyebrows and the same smooth skin as Maria, with the same freckles.

Are you going to change as you get older? Zoe silently asked her reflection. Of course she would. But how much? And in what way? Zoe was curious to find out what would happen to her, and a little scared, but she knew there was nothing she could do about it. She sighed to herself as she walked away from the mirror – she was just growing up.

CHAPTER TWO

The Album

'Your face looks really funny in this one. You look like a little ghost.'

'It's the light, silly! The stage lights always create that effect if you're not wearing make-up. And we aren't allowed to wear make-up, as you well know,' said Zoe.

It was Saturday afternoon. She and Leda were leafing through the photo album at Zoe's gran's house.

'But look – I don't look like a ghost. Mum did my make-up secretly,' admitted Leda.

'Really? And no one noticed?'

'Madame Olenska was too nervous about the recital

to notice it. She was convinced that it was going to be a disaster. Do you remember she used to call us the clumsy class? She said she'd never had such a disorganised group of first years, *mon Dieu*!

Leda raised the back of her hand to her forehead and threw back her head in a good impression of Madame in her more theatrical moments. Zoe laughed; she could laugh now, but thinking back to that first year at Ballet Academy, so long ago, she couldn't imagine having even a little giggle like that at the time. She'd been far too scared.

Mum and Dad tried not to place too much emphasis on Zoe's success at the Academy. She knew they didn't want Maria and Sara to be jealous (although they were perfectly capable of becoming jealous all on their own). So at home there was only one framed photograph of Zoe in her first, very simple black leotard, next to one of Maria in a swimming costume and one of Sara in a ski suit. All three of them were the same age in the photos but they didn't look at all alike, partly because of the clothes they were wearing, but also partly because that was the way it had always been.

The other photos of Zoe's life at the Academy were hidden away inside sealed envelopes in the bottom of the chest of drawers on the landing, divided up year by year, recital by recital. Sometimes Zoe and her mum looked at them, usually when they added the latest envelope, but only if there was nobody else at home.

But now she and Leda were at her gran's house – a wonderful place where they could do the things that they weren't allowed to do anywhere else: eat ten sweets in one go, watch two movies in a row, slide down the shiny marble hall in their socks, and, of course, leaf through the ballet photo album that Gran kept. She had added a sentence of her own here and there or a verse of poetry, a pastel drawing of a crown of flowers or a pair of pink ballet shoes.

Zoe thought her gran was amazing. When Zoe sometimes went over to her house with Leda to look at the photos, her gran never fussed over them. She brought some tea for them with a little snack (finger biscuits, covered with delicious chocolate) and then disappeared, leaving them alone with only one request: 'I don't want any fingerprints on my photo album.'

So they munched up the biscuits first, then they licked their chocolatey fingers clean, like a couple of cats, and started to leaf through the album. The photograph of the first recital – the one with Zoe the little ghost and Leda with her secret make-up – revealed a great deal about that first year at the Academy.

Zoe vaguely remembered the entrance exams for the Academy. It had been summer. She had a memory of dark, heavy blinds struggling to keep out the sunlight from a large room and lots of little girls like her moving to a river of music.

'Move around, do what you want, run, jump,' they were instructed. 'You're free to move as you like.'

She always did that, at home, whenever any music started, whether it was on the CD player, radio or television, so doing it again came naturally to her, even in front of those strangers. Besides, the girls thought that it was a game, although the medical examination afterwards wasn't much fun.

Then, one evening, not long before they went on holiday to the seaside (Zoe could remember it well, because she was wandering around the house in bare feet, carrying her new pink rubber ring with both hands), Mum announced, 'They've accepted you, sweetheart. You're starting at Ballet Academy in September.'

And her mum and sister and dad all gave her a big hug.

And that was that. In September, there had been so many new things: the first year at the Academy was also Zoe's first time at a big school, with all the effort of obeying rules, sitting still for such a long time, paying attention and concentrating. Fortunately, she already knew how to read and write a bit, so that had been quite easy.

Then there were the dance classes – the wonderful lessons that taught you how to be a ballerina. When they gave her the black leotard, more plain than the plainest swimming costume, she was a bit disappointed. The shoes lived up to expectations though: they were made of supple leather, pale pink, with ribbons to lace them up tightly and securely. They were absolutely beautiful.

She had been a bit disappointed by the lessons as well to start with – well, disappointed with the exercises they did at any rate. Repeating the same movements, again, and again, and again was dull and she didn't feel anything like the ballerinas she had seen on the stage.

The very first thing Madame Olenska had said was, 'Work, work, work. To be good, you have to put in a lot of hard work. Do not look at yourselves in the mirror; all you'll see will be clumsy little geese. *Think.* Your arms have to think, your legs have to think, your feet have to think . . .'

Little Zoe had thought that the idea of feet thinking was very strange. What would a foot think? That the wrinkle in its sock was bothering it? That it would like its nails painted blue? That it would really like to go around bare all the time, like in the summer, when it was bare nearly all day long. Then she stopped thinking about it, because she was too busy watching and listening to their teacher, and at some point since then she had realised that her feet really did seem to be thinking for themselves, because they knew what to do without Zoe using her head to tell them. And slowly everything had become easier.

Easier, but not easy. In the afternoons, when she got home after school and ballet lessons, sometimes she had been so tired that she curled up on the carpet and fell asleep in front of the television. Sometimes she hadn't woken up until the next morning, in her bed and miraculously wearing her pyjamas.

Her mum used to say, 'This morning you'll have to have a super-big breakfast. I tried to wake you for dinner yesterday, but I couldn't.'

But gradually her body got used to the hard work, and she stopped falling asleep like a little baby. She was growing up.

'Take a look at this one. You can tell you didn't know which direction to go in.'

Leda's voice brought her back to her gran's house, to the here and now.

'And look at you,' teased Zoe, pointing to another picture. 'You're staring at your feet! Were you worried they were going to come loose and dance off somewhere by themselves?'

To be honest, all ten of those little girls in black leotards had looked rather lost – they were so small against the vast darkness of the stage. Nearly all of them had their eyes glued on a point to the right of the picture, the spot where Madame Olenska had stood, well hidden from the audience, attempting to guide them with her hand gestures. It hadn't done much good, though, judging from the puzzled looks on their faces. Only one girl looked straight ahead, serious and confident: Laila – easily recognisable and already perfect.

'Who was that?' asked Zoe. She pointed at a chubby girl with very black hair. 'She looks like Olivia the piglet.' Zoe felt a bit mean saying it, but it was a harsh truth. The girl looked a little too podgy to be a ballerina.

'Her name was . . . Beatrice, I think. Yes, Beatrice, and the other one's Julia. Don't you remember?' Leda asked. 'Julia used to cry all the time.'

'Oh, that's right.'

Zoe remembered that sometimes she'd felt like crying as well, especially that first year. All it took was a cutting remark from Madame Olenska, or one of her nasty looks, and it took a huge effort to hold back her tears. Everything would go blurred for a few seconds, like she'd plunged underwater. Then she'd give a big sigh and tried to carry on as normal.

'Both of them left at the end of the first year,' Leda said. 'We didn't.'

They looked at each other and smiled. They hadn't left. They were still there. They'd made it – so far.

Zoe hadn't been friends with Leda straightaway. At first, she'd had to concentrate so hard on everything she needed to do that she'd really had no time to think about anything else. The other children all looked more or less the same to Zoe, particularly in ballet class. The boys and girls wore the same leotards, although the boys wore black shoes, while the girls wore pink. The girls had to do their hair in the same severe style which made them all look identical. In the first year, it was two buns, one on each side, which were really difficult to keep up – the first few times Zoe remembered their buns bristled with hairpins like little spiky hedgehogs.

And then, after a few weeks, Leda had come forward to say hello and shyly but surely had become her friend.

'Do you remember when you gave me that pink *Hello Kitty* rubber?' Zoe asked her fondly. 'You'd already used it a bit, but I really liked it.'

'You kept looking at it all the time, but you never said anything to me. You looked at the rubber more than you looked at me,' smiled Leda.

'But you loved it so much. You even asked me if I'd still let you use it sometimes.'

'It was a present from my dad,' said Leda.

Zoe already knew that, but she understood that Leda

was repeating it deliberately, just to hear the words. Her dad had left two years ago. Now he had another family and a little boy who Leda called 'my little brother'. He was of course, but they saw so little of each other that he was more like an idea of a little brother than a real one. At least, that's what Zoe thought, but she'd never say so. Leda was already upset enough about it, and saying anything would just upset her more.

Since that day with the pink rubber, they'd been inseparable. They'd managed to switch seats so they could sit together in classes; had helped each other when they'd had to learn joined-up writing and how to fold their white socks properly above their tightly laced ballet shoes; together they'd learned to cope with Madame Olenska's sharp comments and frowns; they'd comforted each other when they were tired or disappointed with themselves; and defended the other from the doses of spitefulness that Laila dished out every day – she left a slippery path of hurt trailing behind her wherever she went.

Now they were growing up, Zoe suspected that things would not be so simple. It would take more than giving a *Hello Kitty* rubber as a present, lending a hair ribbon, or giving a look of support to cheer them up. Zoe, who had always been such a chatterbox, saying what she thought without thinking about it too much, had recently found herself biting her tongue.

She was tiptoeing around Leda – not literally of course, but in the sense of avoiding certain topics of conversation. So far, it had worked. But Zoe knew that it wasn't going to work any more when Leda asked her out of the blue, 'Do you think that I'm going to be too tall to be a ballerina?'

They were looking at a photograph of their third-year recital, when five of them were chosen to be little flowers in *Spring*, starring Mariah Simone.

Mariah Simone was in her final year then, one step away from her diploma, but everyone already knew that she was going to be a soloist. You could see it in the way she moved, in her gracefulness and the natural way she danced. And they, the little flowers (Leda and Zoe, of course, plus Laila, Sophie and Stephanie), were so nervous at the thought of being on stage with the star. Even the inscrutable Laila had seemed anxious at the time, and her usually impassive expression became almost pleading in the presence of Mariah Simone: look at me, *see me*, let me become like you.

They had really enjoyed themselves though – they finally had real tutus, pink and green ones that were short and layered, and headdresses made of little silk flowers. The steps were simple (Madame Olenska had deliberately chosen them to make sure there was no chance of mistakes) and they'd learned the dance quickly. The show had been a triumph. All that applause, and it was finally for them as well!

But none of that mattered now – it was in the distant past. At the moment, Leda was concerned about whether she would become a swan after all. They both knew that ballerinas must be small – *petite*, as Madame Olenska said. It was just too hard to find a male dancer who was capable of lifting a tall ballerina. And dieting wouldn't affect your height – if you were too tall, your bones and muscles simply weighed too much.

So, the moment that Zoe had been trying to avoid had arrived . . . and she didn't know what to say. Leda's dad was well over six feet tall – he was practically a giant. Her mum wasn't small either. Unless there was some midget amongst her grandparents and great-grandparents to balance it out, Leda was destined to become pretty tall.

So, what should she do? Tell the truth? Lie? Zoe hesitated for a moment too long and Leda spoke before she could reply.

'I see. I guess you're going to tell me I can always go into modern dance. But I couldn't give a sausage about modern dance.'

Zoe started. Leda was always so polite that 'couldn't give a sausage' sounded like the most shocking of swear-words coming from her mouth. Leda didn't notice, she wasn't even looking at Zoe. She just continued staring at the album.

'I've only ever wanted to be a classical ballerina. I don't want to end up as a chorus girl – they're just second-rate showgirls to me.'

Leda was talking quietly, without anger, without agitation, as though these were things she'd repeated to herself again and again. Zoe couldn't think of anything better to do than hug her really tight, without saying a single word. Leda always had a scent of camomile about her that was so beautiful and gentle – just like Leda.

'Have you finished your trip down memory lane now, you two?' Gran's voice interrupted them. 'My goodness me, only eleven years old and here you are brooding over the past!'

Gran entered the room without making a sound, as though she had glided in. She was carrying a tray of flapjacks. Zoe knew that her gran had sensed that something was wrong, but she didn't ask the girls any questions. She put down the tray, sat in the armchair, and turned to Leda.

'May I?' Then she took the album from Leda's hands, turned the pages and stopped. 'Here,' she said. 'This one's my favourite. You can see that you're happy.'

It was the photograph from the last year's recital – the final shot, when they were taking a bow. When you curtsied, you always had to smile: it was one of Madame Olenska's thousand rules. But the fourteen smiles printed on the glossy paper were all different and distinctive. Zoe didn't need to look at the picture to remember it. In the first row were the ten girls, with the four boys standing behind. She was the second from the left and was laughing, rather than smiling, as Madame Olenska hadn't failed to point out when they had all first seen the photograph together, on the last day of term.

'You look like a hyena, Zoe,' she'd said. 'All those teeth on display. Too many teeth.'

Zoe had run over to the mirror to take a look at herself, imitating that smile. She thought she just had normal teeth, not too many at all. And anyway hyenas sneered and were mean. When the photo was taken, Zoe had just been happy. Leda was laughing a bit too much as well, but in her sweet, shy way, which could never, ever be compared to a hyena's grin. If a fawn laughed, it would do it like that. And Leda was laughing because her dad was in the audience.

Laila's smile was perfect. Zoe had to admit that she was very good. She'd also performed a short *pas de deux* with Matthew, who'd studied at the Paris Opera School and had amazing technique. She had every reason to smile.

'And what are you going to do for this year's recital?' Gran asked.

Neither of them answered. They were too busy munching away – there were still a few delicious flapjacks to sink their teeth into. After a long silence, Zoe finally swallowed her mouthful and licked her sugary lips.

'*The Dance Class*. That's what our dance is called. It's based on a famous painting,' she told her gran.

'That's right – by Degas,' said Gran.

Zoe continued. 'There's a teacher, and the others all do what you do in a real lesson. Some of them make mistakes and get told off; some of them are good and the teacher praises them . . .'

'The usual things, you know,' interrupted Leda. 'The kind of things that happen every day.'

'Let me guess,' said Gran. 'The teacher will be played by —'

'Laila,' Zoe and Leda chorused.

'Well, that's all right, isn't it? It must be a really boring part.'

'Yes, but she'll have a cane,' said Zoe.

'And of course she has to show everyone the right way to do things,' explained Leda.

'It'd be funnier if she had to dress up like Madame Olenska,' smiled Zoe.

All three of them laughed, imagining Laila wrapped

up in one of the dramatic kaftans with matching turban that the headmistress loved so much.

'Actually, she's annoyed because she doesn't get to wear a tutu. She'll be sobbing her heart out,' said Zoe.

'We're the ones who should be feeling sorry for ourselves. If we're pretending to have a dance lesson, we'll have to wear those black leotards again like we did in the first year,' said Leda, grimacing

'Not necessarily,' said Gran. 'In the painting the girls all have proper tutus. They're beautiful.'

Zoe didn't say a word, but her eyes were twinkling. Demetra, the head costume-maker, was very fond of Zoe, and had shown her the design for their recital costumes. Admittedly, the design wasn't for a prima ballerina's tutu, but it was beautiful: a pearl-grey leotard with a circle of soft tulle, short at the sides and edged with a subtle silver trim, chalk-white tights, white shoes, a silver band for their hair. An absolute delight. But it was still a secret. She'd only shown Zoe because they got on so well.

As they were walking home together from Gran's house, Zoe felt something needed to be said. It didn't seem right to her to leave the earlier conversation as it was, half finished, silenced by the sweetness of the flapjacks.

'You could always be a model,' Zoe suggested suddenly. 'You're so beautiful that designers will be falling over themselves to have you wear their clothes.'

Leda didn't answer immediately. They carried on walking for a while. Zoe knew that Leda would speak when she was ready.

'It's just that it doesn't seem to have lasted long enough,' Leda said then. 'All of this, I mean. Studying dance was always a bit like a dream for me. Ever since I was three years old, I've been telling people I'm going to be a ballerina when I grow up. And when they accepted me at the Academy, I was over the moon, because it was what I really wanted, you know? I always knew that there was a possibility that I might not actually go all the way and my dream might not come true – there are so many ballerinas much better than me. But I thought that I could go on trying and being special, at least until I was eighteen or nineteen, and then maybe decide to do something else . . . go to university perhaps, you know, be normal. But if I carry on growing like this, you know what Madame Olenska will say . . .'

'"Dead wood must be cut away immediately",' recited Zoe, glumly quoting one of their teacher's harsher sayings.

'She doesn't think twice about throwing out anyone who's not making progress, or won't succeed. She says it's better that way.'

'And maybe she's right,' said Zoe, very quietly.

There was a long pause. The only sound that could be

heard were their slow, slow footsteps.

'And I agree,' Leda said after a while. 'But it might mean that I'm going to have to become normal a lot sooner than I hoped.'

They didn't say another word. They parted with a short, firm hug, in front of Zoe's house. Zoe couldn't think about anything else all that evening apart from Leda's quiet sadness and her shattered dreams.

CHAPTER THREE

The Mysteries of Madame Olenska

'I'm scared of her,' Leda said.

It was the following Friday night and Zoe and Leda were watching a strange Japanese film called *Princess Mononoke.* It was about a wolf-girl trying to defend her forest against progress. The story was complicated and there seemed to be a lot of blood, but the animation was stunning.

'Scared of who? Lady Eboshi in the film?' asked Zoe.

But she knew very well who her friend was talking about. Madame Olenska.

Zoe was delighted that Leda had agreed to come over for a film and supper. They'd spent a long time talking about Leda's future at Ballet Academy.

'I don't think that Madame Olenska will throw you out,' Zoe said, and she meant it.

'Why not? She's already done it to at least, let's see . . . five, six, seven girls. Seven girls in five years.'

'Yes, but you're different. You're good. You're just a bit too tall.'

She sighed. 'I'm really scared though that one day she'll call me over and tell me that I've grown too tall and that there's no point in continuing if I've got no future as a ballerina – that it'd be a waste of time. She'll say that if I go, I'll free up a place for someone who does have a chance. You know, it'd be a real tragedy for Mum.' Leda's voice trailed off.

Leda's mum had studied dance when she was a little girl. But she'd lived in a small town and the school was nothing special, she just danced for fun – her parents would never have allowed her to go and study at a proper dance school, far away from home. So it remained a dream – one that came true for Leda.

Zoe had asked her own mum about it once. 'Why did you make me study dance?' she had asked her.

'I'm not the one making you study dance. You're the one who wants to do it,' her mum had answered calmly.

'Yes, I know, but you took me to the entrance exam.'

'Of course I did. Have you ever heard of a girl of five

signing up for a swimming course, or an art class or dance lessons by herself? I just watched you. I could see that you enjoyed moving. So I created an opportunity for you. If you'd got bored or if your dad or I had realised it wasn't the right thing for you, that it was too tiring or it was making you unhappy, we'd have made you stop straightaway. But you just liked it more and more, and I think you still enjoy it, don't you? Or am I wrong? Is there something you want to tell me?'

'No, no,' Zoe had reassured her. 'I really do still enjoy it. I was just thinking about Leda's mum. You know, sometimes I have the feeling that she cares even more about all of this dance stuff than Leda does. It's as though she wants Leda to think that it's the most important thing in the world.'

'Perhaps you're right,' her mum had said. 'But as long as Leda still cares about it, things can carry on as they are. And it seems to me that Leda really likes what she's doing. Isn't that right?'

Zoe knew that it was. While it was Leda's mother's passion, nothing mattered more to Leda either.

Zoe watched as her friend forced a smile, trying to push her worries away.

'I don't think I'm the only one who's scared of Madame Olenska though. Do you think she's always been like that?' asked Leda.

'Like what?' Zoe replied.

'I don't know, that *mean*.'

'Maybe she was in love with a male ballet dancer who ran off to America with another woman,' mused Zoe.

'A dancer? Or maybe a choreographer. Or a conductor – one of those with the really messy hair, who look mad, like Einstein,' Leda suggested.

'And he chose his career instead of love. And she decided to come to the West by herself to forget him, but she still thinks about him all the time.'

'Definitely. And that's why she's so awful. Because it's a kind of subconscious revenge,' Leda went on.

'And we poor little lambs are her innocent victims.'

'I don't know about innocent. Sometimes she's right to get angry. It's not as though we always listen to her . . .'

'Yes, I know. But she shouldn't have a go at us in front of everyone. It's so humiliating,' Zoe said.

'True, but just imagine if she called you into her office by yourself instead! I'd be so terrified that I'd die of terror on the spot.'

'Come on, she's not as bad as she seems. Mum always says you shouldn't judge people by appearances,' said Zoe, turning back to the film.

Zoe had good reason to suggest that Madame Olenska wasn't as bad as she seemed. It was because of something that had happened three years ago, which had remained a secret between them.

At the end of the second year, Zoe had been doing really badly for the previous few months. She didn't know why. Maybe she was a bit tired, maybe a little jealous of Maria at home, who was an adorable little girl, doted on by her mum and dad. Maybe it was just the effort of having to live up to everyone's high expectations. Zoe was usually so conscientious. Maybe she was tired of being the usual Zoe and was looking for a bit of attention, which meant her own attention levels went out of the window and her feet did whatever they felt like doing.

So, one day, she really did end up all on her own in Madame Olenska's office. At the end of the lesson, the headmistress had placed a hand on her shoulder and said to her, 'Come with me.'

Then she shunted Zoe down the corridors like a supermarket trolley, a turn to the right, a turn to the left, to the right again, through the labyrinth of the Academy. She led her through a green painted door and then it was just the two of them, all on their own.

Zoe had never been in Madame Olenska's office before. It was a big room, full of light, with very high ceilings and long white curtains that blew around like sails in the breeze. There were bookshelves from floor to ceiling on one wall; another wall was covered with big black-and-white photographs; along the third wall there was a large, impressive desk with a green leather surface and a lamp with a shade that looked like a glass mosaic. Zoe remembered wishing it was on, so she could see all those colours illuminated from inside.

'Sit down,' Madame Olenska said.

Zoe tried to relax, to think of something calming, but it was pointless. She sat down on the edge of one of the two tall wooden chairs, the one furthest away from the desk. Madame Olenska walked around the desk and sat down in her chair. Her back, as always, was as straight as a rod. Her twinkling eyes were so terribly blue. She laced her fingers together and her many rings sparkled. Strange, thought Zoe, given the way she always said, 'No jewellery, girls' and sent them back to the changing room if they forgot to take off even the tiniest of earrings.

'So,' she said. 'I want to tell you a story.'

A story? Zoe didn't even have time to be astonished – she'd been so ready for a telling off, or even being told she'd have to leave the Academy. Madame Olenska opened a drawer and took something out. She placed the something directly in front of Zoe. It was a black-and-white photograph in a reddish leather frame. The photograph showed a thin girl with a big smile, her hair in a bun on top of her head and a fairytale tutu –

one of the wide, stiff ones that every girl at the Academy dreamed of wearing.

'That's me when I was your age,' she said.

Zoe was astounded, but she tried not to let it show. Of course, Madame Olenska must have been a little girl once, at some time and in some world. But the girl in the picture was so . . . so normal, that was it. It seemed incredible that she'd grown up into the fierce teacher Zoe knew.

'When I was your age, I'd just started at the Dance School in Leningrad. That's what the city was called back then – but now it's St Petersberg. I came from the countryside, and my parents had made huge sacrifices so that I could have dance lessons. I had private lessons from a man who used to dance at the Bolshoi Ballet, but had returned to the place of his birth. It wasn't a beautiful practice room like here, it was a minuscule apartment of just two rooms. In the practice room he had installed an enormous mirror on one entire wall, with a barre.'

Madame Olenska had a strangely sweet expression on her face as she spoke. It was almost dreamy.

'Nikolai Grigoriev was an exceptional teacher,' Madame Olenska continued. 'In two years he taught me what other girls learn in five. And he prepared me for the entrance exams.'

Here we go, thought Zoe, *I can tell the rest of the story myself. Of course they accepted her immediately. In fact, she was the first girl to win a place. She stayed at the top of her class for all of her years at school. That's how it must have been.* However, what Madame Olenska said next was a complete surprise.

'I didn't pass the exam.'

Zoe looked at Madame Olenska with eyes like saucers.

'I was first on the waiting list. Then, two months later, a girl had to leave. So they called me. And that's the end of the story. You may go.'

It seemed more like the beginning of the story to Zoe thought, but she didn't dare say that out loud. She stood up, gave a quick curtsy and left the room.

For the rest of the day – on her own in the corridor, during the gym lesson at the end of the day and all the way back home, holding on to her mum's hand (she was little then and her mum used to take her to school and pick her up every day) – Zoe wondered why Madame Olenska had told her that story. Zoe finally realised that Madame Olenska hadn't given her a lecture or a warning because the story was enough of a threat in itself: if you don't work hard enough, someone else will take your place. But it could mean a lot of other things too: that you couldn't always be the best, for example. Or maybe you had to *become* the best – that was the most important thing.

Anyway, since then she'd seen Madame Olenska with different eyes. And occasionally she still thought about the story – about that girl in the old photograph with the big smile. Was she happy? Proud? Satisfied? Or was she, deep down, really scared that she'd got what she wanted now, but that she was going to have to hold on to it tightly with both hands?

Zoe glanced at Leda, who was absorbed in the film once more. Madame Olenska's story was one of the few things in her life that Zoe had never told Leda about, but she still didn't intend to tell her now. It was nice to have a friend you could tell things to, but that didn't mean that you had to tell them *everything*. It was important to keep some things to yourself. Besides, it didn't seem the right thing to say. It was clear that Leda was a bit depressed, and that the thought of leaving was really tormenting her. But Zoe couldn't help, except to be as reassuring as possible. If Leda was going to stay, she had to trust in her own abilities, and that was something Zoe couldn't do for her, even if she wanted to.

Mum ordered in a really delicious pizza after they watched the DVD, and there was ice cream for pudding. Maria got tomato all over her face, then dived into her bowl of ice cream as if she were starving. Sara was unusually cheerful. Her netball team had won their match, so there was something to celebrate. The evening was good fun. When he got home, Dad pretended to be horrified and said, 'Five women? I don't think I'm going to survive this!'

But in spite of the pizza and everything else, Zoe knew that Leda was still gloomy. Then Zoe had a flash of inspiration. There *was* something she could do to help her friend!

The next Monday, after school, instead of heading for the main entrance, Zoe waited for everyone else to leave. Then she made her way through the corridors (so strange, empty and silent) and stopped at the door to Madame Olenska's office.

She knocked twice, politely.

'Come in.'

Zoe entered. No curtsy this time – curtsies in ordinary clothes looked ridiculous.

'Good evening, Madame Olenska. Could I speak to you?'

Madame Olenska gestured toward a chair, silently.

Zoe sat on the edge of the chair, just like she had that first time. She decided that if she wanted to be convincing she had to at least pretend to be confident. She made herself as comfortable as possible, leaning against the rigid back of the chair, which somehow seemed to both support and encourage her.

'I want to tell you a story,' Zoe began. 'Once upon a time there was a girl who wanted to be a classical ballerina when she grew up.'

Madame Olenska stared at her, arching one of her eyebrows. *How does she do that?* Zoe wondered, but didn't allow herself to be intimidated.

'But at a certain point she started growing and growing and growing. She was very worried, because she knew that the classical ballet companies don't have space for ballerinas who are too tall. And because she was so worried, she became distracted in lessons and made mistakes, and she wasn't as good as she always had been.'

She paused to breathe. Zoe knew she'd been talking too quickly, the words pouring out of her mouth like a river. Madame Olenska watched her with considerable curiosity and also something else – something that Zoe couldn't quite figure out. Amusement? Irritation? It was hard to say.

'But then a very famous choreographer made a new ballet, a ballet that conquered the world. It was called *Symphony for Tall Girls*, so there were only tall ballerinas on stage. One of them, the soloist, had said farewell to her pointe shoes because she realised that she could no longer use them and she hung them from a nail on the wall. But then she found a teacher who made her dance barefoot and free, and taught her to use her height to create beautiful shadows with her body, and lots of new jumps and athletic moves, and the other tall girls all joined her, and a new show was born. It was so wonderful that everyone went to see it and they all applauded like mad.'

There was silence because Zoe had finished saying what she had to say. Now it was Madame Olenska's turn to speak, or so Zoe hoped.

Finally, she broke the silence. 'Once,' she said slowly and seriously, 'I told you a story. Now you've told me a story. I'd say that we're even. Enough stories, Zoe. From now on, we work.'

And she gently tilted her head to one side and clasped her hands together in front of her.

Zoe stood up, said goodbye and left the office. She wasn't so naive as to think that things would change just because she'd spoken to Madame Olenska, or to think that Madame hadn't noticed Leda's misery by herself. But at least she'd done *something*, and now she'd done it, she felt calmer.

The headmistress was a enigmatic woman, but that was why Zoe liked her. As she went home, she thought again about the Russian girl in that other story. If she was from the countryside and had gone to study in St Petersburg, she must have had to live away from her parents.

There were only a few students who lived at the

Academy during term-time, and they were all older. Zoe thought it must be hard living at school. She didn't know if she could cope with that, no matter how much she loved dancing. How had that Russian girl had coped, she wondered, and how had she felt, all alone and away from her parents?

CHAPTER FOUR

Poor Laila

Stomp, stomp, stomp, stomp! '*Phweehaarghooo!*'

Laila's elephant impression was really bad. The noises she made were terrible. The only thing she was doing really well were the movements. You had to admit that she moved beautifully – she could make her body do whatever she wanted it to.

Zoe was seething. Laila's impression of an elephant had started when she'd walked into the room with Leda, and was obviously meant as an insult to Leda. It was the final straw. Zoe couldn't stand it when Laila behaved like that – they'd all endured her teasing over the years but now she'd gone too far. Leda just walked on to the changing rooms, but Zoe could see her eyes were glistening. Zoe would have gone over to Laila and given her a shove –maybe even a shove and a kick – to make her stop, if she could have got away with it. Two kicks were what she really deserved.

But the rules of the Academy were clear. They weren't written rules – it wasn't as though there was a notice hanging up somewhere in the school saying anyone who kicked their fellow students would be expelled. But it was something that everyone knew. Kicks (and shoves) were not tolerated at the Academy, and not the sort of behaviour expected from ballerinas – they should be putting their energies into doing a *port de bras* or an *arabesque* instead.

Zoe was tempted to lift up her leg in a perfect *arabesque* and accidentally on purpose poke the tip of her shoe in Laila's eye. Oh, if only, if only!

But then she had another idea. As she put on her ballet shoes in the changing room in preparation for the next lesson, she was already contemplating a more subtle and satisfying revenge.

In the changing room the next day, Leda came over to Zoe. 'Have you noticed how strangely Laila's acting today?' Leda whispered.

Zoe looked up, then back down at her laces. 'You're right,' she said, wrapping them tightly, but not too tightly, around her ankle. 'Her face is all red. Maybe she's coming down with something.'

Then, in the lesson, something extraordinary happened. Madame Olenska told Laila off.

'Laila, please, a little more attention!'

It certainly wasn't a proper telling-off, but it was enough to make her turn crimson, because it was something that had never happened before. Laila never, ever got a reprimand. All she ever heard from Madame Olenska was, 'Yes, that's fine', 'Well done' or 'Correct'.

It really was quite an exceptional event and everyone was completely astounded. Leda shot a glance at Zoe in the mirror, who was just about managing to keep a straight face. Then Madame Olenska clapped her hands three times.

'What is going on, children? Please try to concentrate.' And the lesson continued.

But thanks to the huge mirror they practised in front of, Zoe could keep an eye on Laila, and she could see that Laila was directing increasingly insistent glances in one particular direction, and that direction was Roberto.

Roberto was Italian, he'd studied at the La Scala Ballet School in Milan, then his dad had moved to England for work and the family followed him. The

Academy obviously accepted him straightaway. He was really good-looking, with lovely deep brown hair and pale skin. He had blue eyes, was tall, slim, and he was also a very good dancer. The only problem was that his English wasn't very good yet, so he hardly ever said anything, and because he was a little shy too (you could see that from a mile off), he tended to spend all of his time with the boys.

Lucas, whom Zoe liked best out of the boys (but just as a friend, of course), said that Roberto was nice. In which case, he was practically perfect. Perhaps that was why Laila had started flirting with him the moment he arrived, with the result that he retreated even further into his shell.

When the lesson was over, Paula said to Laila, 'You really fancy him, don't you? I saw the way you were looking at him . . .'

'What? What on *earrrth* are you talking about?' Laila retorted, with a French 'r' that sounded as long as three 'r's in a row.

'I'm talking about Roberto. You must be really head over heels if you managed to get told off by Madame. But he doesn't even know you exist, does he?'

Laila didn't answer, but just smiled smugly to herself and carried on getting changed. Strange, considering that she usually had to have the last word on everything, and a cutting one at that. Leda looked at Zoe, expecting her to add some remark of her own, but Zoe shook her head. She smiled too, and looked down at the floor.

As they were going home the next day, Leda took Zoe by the arm. 'Guess what?' she cried. 'When I got to the changing room today there was no one else there, just Laila. And do you know what she was doing? She was reading a crumpled piece of paper. When she saw me, she screwed it up into a ball and hid her hand behind her back. I pretended not to notice, but she was behaving so strangely that she didn't even make those elephant noises at me. I think Paula's right: it has to be Roberto. But I didn't think he liked Laila – I mean, she's so nasty . . . but he was the one who wrote her that note, I'm sure of it.'

Zoe didn't answer. Instead, she changed the subject. 'Do you fancy coming to my house to watch a film? I've got a new one. It's called *Spirited Away*. It's by the same director as *Princess Mononoke*.'

Another day passed. It was lunchtime and the students in the junior school were all in the playground. The boys in Zoe's year were together, in a group, as usual. Unusually, though, they weren't playing football. Instead they seemed to be busy discussing something.

Suddenly, Laila, who was sitting as usual by herself on the bench beneath the horse chestnut tree, got up, walked over to the group of boys, stopped right in front of Roberto, directed a sweet smile at him and said in a loud voice, 'Yes.'

Everyone, including the girls, looked at her in astonishment. Laila never talked to anyone – or rather, she did talk, but just to make mean remarks that didn't deserve any kind of response. And 'yes' wasn't some spiteful remark, so this really was an extraordinary turn of events.

Roberto looked most amazed of all. He stared at Laila for a moment and then, in his foreign accent, he asked her, 'Yes what?'

'You asked me if I wanted to be your girlfriend. Well, the answer's yes,' said Laila, her smile a little more fixed now and less sweet.

Roberto looked at her as if she'd gone mad.

Lucas, clearly thinking he hadn't understood what she'd said, tried to explain to him, speaking very slowly. 'She said you asked her —'

Roberto interrupted him. 'I got that. But I don't want a girlfriend. And I certainly don't want *her* to be my girlfriend.'

And he looked at Laila, very seriously. He almost seemed to be feeling a little sorry for her.

Laila whirled round to glare at the girls. 'You're going

to pay for this!' she hissed, then stomped back inside.

Leda came over to Zoe. 'Somebody must have played a joke on her,' she said. 'Someone must have put a fake note in her bag . . .' She stole a glance at her friend.

'And she fell for it,' said Zoe, looking straight back at Leda.

'Well, it serves her right,' said Leda, smiling.

'Just for once, she's the victim!'

'You're right,' said Leda. 'She deserved it.'

Lucas came over to the two of them. He gave them a big grin. 'So, whose idea was that little joke?' he asked and looked at Zoe. 'I've got a good idea who it might have been.'

'It wasn't me,' said Zoe.

'You sure?' insisted Lucas.

'I'd tell you if I'd done it,' said Zoe, smiling. 'Really I would.'

Lucas looked at her, and believed her. 'OK, but whoever it was, they did a good thing. Laila's really mean to all of you girls and it was about time someone showed her what it's like.'

'But she's not mean to the boys, is she?' said Leda.

'No, you're right,' replied Lucas. 'Maybe she doesn't think of us as rivals. You lot are all potential competition for our ambitious little *mademoiselle*.'

'Let's talk about something else,' said Zoe. 'We've

already wasted enough time. Break's over in ten minutes. How about a quick game of prisoner ball?'

'Boys against girls? Definitely!' said Lucas, and he ran to get the others.

'You're all sweating and puffing like a herd of wildebeest,' said Madame Olenska, looking at her class at the beginning of the lesson. 'You know I don't like you to play violent games before you come to me. All of you should calm down immediately. We need to concentrate on our work. Laila, have you forgotten how to brush your hair?'

That really was the last straw for Laila. It was true, though. Laila's bun was completely lopsided and about to collapse, and there were strands of hair hanging around her neck. She was completely red in the face, but not, like the others, because of the game. Laila had blotches all over her face, like a badly drawn map, and her eyes had bright red rings around them. *It's as if she has an allergy to something,* Zoe thought to herself. *Probably jokes.*

But, Madame Olenska's comment was more than she could bear and Laila did something that no one had ever dared to do in class before – she left. She just left the room without asking permission, and the only reason she didn't slam the door was because it was the kind that creaked on its hinges, then slowly swung to and closed itself.

The eyes of all the students moved from the door to

Madame Olenska, who didn't say a word, but just pursed her lips.

'Now we shall begin,' she said, and she gave a signal to the pianist. 'First position! And one, and two, and three, and four . . .'

When everyone went through to the changing room after the lesson, there was no sign of Laila. Her clothes bag was empty and her shoes had disappeared from underneath the bench. She had gone.

Leda crouched down beside Zoe and whispered, 'It *was* you, wasn't it?'

'What was me?' asked Zoe, but she knew very well what Leda meant.

'Who played that joke on Laila. Hiding the fake note from Roberto in her bag. It was you, and you did it because she keeps making fun of me.'

'No, Leda. It wasn't me.' Zoe looked into her friend's eyes.

Leda looked at her quizzically. Zoe sighed. She lowered her gaze, then looked again at Leda, who was waiting expectantly.

'It wasn't me – honestly. Although I wish it had been me, in a way,' Zoe admitted. 'It really gets me mad when she's mean to you, and it upsets me even when it's someone else she's picking on. And before, in the playground, when she made such a fool of herself in front of Roberto and all the other boys, I was really happy. But now I'm not happy at all, because leaving the class like that is really serious. Laila's risking so much. You know that too. And I'm wondering . . . if it was worth it, just for a joke. I had a plan but someone else got there first. She must have been really hurt to react like that.'

By now, Zoe and Leda were completely dressed and the other girls had all gone.

'Well, if it wasn't you, it must have been Paula,' whispered Leda, looking at her feet.

'I don't think it really matters,' said Zoe.

'You're right,' said Leda. 'But, it's not as if I really care when Laila makes fun of me.'

'That's not true, and you know it,' said Zoe, smiling reassuringly. 'You certainly do care. And you get all upset, even when you know that her comments are just stupid. But you're not on your own: you've always got me to cheer you up. Laila's only got herself.'

'Don't tell me you're feeling sorry for her now,' Leda exclaimed, almost surprised.

'That's not what I'm saying. I just feel a bit weird about it, that's all.'

Zoe stood up and pulled on her rucksack and Leda did the same. They walked home together, in silence, each with her own thoughts.

* * *

That evening, Zoe felt terrible. She really had enjoyed the joke. At that moment in the playground, she really *had* wished that she had been the one to have the idea. But only at that moment.

Actually, Zoe admitted to herself, it was a bit of a relief that someone else had got there first, so she hadn't had the chance to use her plan, especially as Laila had taken it so badly.

But there was another reason Zoe felt a bit sorry about the trick on Laila. It was just a bit too close to home. Laila wasn't the only person who liked Roberto – Zoe liked Roberto too. She liked him a lot. She watched him all the time, while trying to make sure she wasn't noticed. She had studied the way his longish hair curled just a little at the back of his neck. She'd noticed his hands, which were a little bony and big for his age. She liked the way he talked slowly, carefully, thinking first about what he was going to say. She liked the fact that he looked a little exotic, and his quietness intrigued her.

So not only did Zoe really feel quite sorry for Laila – she couldn't help wondering how she would feel if someone had played that trick on her. Also, in some strange way that she knew was ridiculous, she felt uneasy because it seemed like Roberto's fault that Laila had been humiliated in front of everyone.

Zoe was standing beside the telephone at home. She didn't know Laila's number. In fact, she hadn't ever dialled it. But Zoe's mum had a piece of paper folded inside her address book with the names and numbers of all of Zoe's classmates on it, and if Zoe wanted to, she could call Laila. She could just ask her how she was, without making a big deal out of it. Or she could dial Roberto's number, and ask him how he was. They were two such different phone calls, both of which were possible, both of which seemed to be waiting for her, calling out to her.

In the end, Zoe left the phone. Instead, she went to her room and shut the door behind her, stretched out on the bed and tried to think of nothing. It was difficult to decide what to do.

Someone knocked. Without waiting, the person flung open the door. It was Maria. She ran in, happy as could be.

'Look what Mummy bought me!' And she showed Zoe her new top, which she was already wearing – white, with a big rainbow on the front.

'She's got tops exactly the same for you and Sara too. Isn't that great?'

Zoe smiled, but her smile was a little forced. She could do without looking like a clone: she did that at school all day. But the top was pretty, and her sister was so happy about the simple rainbow on her T-shirt that Zoe couldn't help but hug her. She squeezed her little sister tight, and breathed in the grapefruit scent of her shampoo. Beneath it she could make out the scent of a little girl who'd been at primary school – a warm mixture of soup and chalk dust.

Maria wriggled free and ran off. 'No soppy stuff, Zoe,' she called back, 'but you can come and play with my dolls if you like.'

Zoe pulled a face. She didn't like Maria's dolls, with their big, wide eyes and heavy make-up. Why couldn't little girls play with baby dolls, like she had, Zoe wondered.

Maria stood waiting for an answer. Zoe finally said yes and Maria dragged her off into her room next door, which was a chaos of cuddly toys and rag dolls and tiny little dolls' accessories with no obvious purpose. On the rug, a small platoon of dolls who all looked like teenagers were waiting for her. 'OK then, let's play,' she said.

Zoe looked at her sister. 'Let's play at being little, while we still can,' she said softly.

In bed later, Zoe tried to remember what she'd been like when she was Maria's age. Memories were strange, Zoe thought. Some of them were so clear that it seemed as though they'd happened only yesterday, but others were buried beneath a mountain of passing time and only surfaced suddenly, when you were least expecting it.

Zoe's earliest memory – at least as far as she could remember – was of a girl with hair flying around her head as someone pushed her high on a swing. The colours in the memory were confused: there was so much sunshine that it reduced everything to silhouettes. Even the little girl was just a silhouette. She just had an idea of a happy little girl laughing and throwing back her head, wanting to be pushed higher and higher.

As she couldn't swing on her own, she must have been very little. Someone had once told Zoe that if you could see a memory from the outside, you were observing someone else, so maybe it was Sara on the swing. Or maybe Zoe had been in a pushchair watching. Now that was a weird thought.

Zoe had once told her mum about the memory. 'We often used to go to the park when you girls were little,' her mum had told her.

Zoe had felt disappointed, because she knew that park so well. She went there with Maria sometimes, and it was the most boring place in the world. It was just a simple public park with patchy grass, a few trees struggling to grow, benches for mums and babysitters, wooden playground equipment to climb and swing on, a kind of castle with a slide, roundabouts made of red and blue metal three swings in a row with rubber seats. Was it possible that her precious first memory was of that place? Zoe would have preferred an enchanted meadow, with a forest nearby, a forest that cast a shadow but didn't scare you because you were out there in bright sunshine and the person with you (Mum? Dad?) protected you and loved you and took care of you, so you could be a little frightened of the forest, but only pretend-frightened, with just a little shiver, because a cuddle was all that was needed to make it go away.

A little girl on a swing. She drew it once as well, but then she crumpled up the paper because her drawing was boring and it made something so wonderful seem so normal.

Zoe's memory of the swing was a vague one, but she did have a very clear memory of her favourite toys. Dolls like Maria's didn't exist back then, but Mum had always tried to steer Zoe toward simple toys, and either Zoe must have been a very obedient little girl or maybe she just liked the same things as her mum, because she remembered a succession of baby dolls, as soft as real babies.

However, Zoe didn't remember any ballerina dolls, or mice or bears dressed as ballerinas – the sort of thing that might have made her decide that ballet was what she wanted to do when she grew up and nothing else would do. Leda's bedroom was packed with that kind of thing, and, as far as Zoe remembered, it always had been. So were the bedrooms of the other girls at school.

There was a whole world of pink out there: sparkling, sprinkled with sequins and stars and hearts, turning dance into a dream world for little girls, where everything was soft and gentle and graceful, and there were only smiles, ribbons, fluttering wings and tutus, steps danced on the tips of your toes, satin, tulle and cashmere.

All these pretty images had no connection at all with the real world of dance, which was serious and strict. In the real world of dance, no one cared whether you had dimples when you smiled or hair held up in a net of silver. In fact, silver hairnets would end up in the rubbish bin, because training was about simplicity. In short, dance was anything but make-believe. When Zoe thought about Maria, who was so small and still so free, she felt a little ache for how life used to be.

CHAPTER FIVE

Secrets

The incident with Laila wasn't going to go away soon – it was the sole topic of conversation in the girls' changing room. In the studio, Laila stood in her corner, on her own as usual. She had regained her poise, but did not meet her classmates' eyes. Any strands of hair suspected of rebellion were pinned into place with an extra hairpin. Her shoe ribbons were as perfect as her steps as she moved from the barre into the centre of the room. You'd have thought everything had returned to normal, but it hadn't. Everyone knew about Laila's crush now.

'It's the springtime, girls,' said Demetra, standing in

the doorway of the costume department, watching them chatter and glance flirtatiously around the room. 'It has the same effect on me . . .' She raised her dreamy eyes, lost in thought.

The girls had done nothing but talk about boys since Laila's crush had been revealed. They talked about this boy being gorgeous, that one being kind, another having a lovely voice . . . Zoe didn't say a word about herself but she did think about it. She found herself imagining Demetra, with her apron and her pins tucked into her blouse and her lively sense of hmour, being in love. Demetra had been married to a stage-hand called Albert for twenty-five years. Could you still be in love after twenty-five years? She'd caught her mum and dad kissing, which was very strange – part of her wished she'd never seen it at all.

Zoe was, however, also listening very carefully to everything that the other girls said. And that was how she knew that:

1. Paula fancied Roberto.

2. Anna couldn't decide between Roberto and Lucas.

3. Stephanie was mad about Victor, who was a couple of years above them, and had been since they were in the first year.

4. Francine would do anything for her next-door neighbour Andrew.

5. Estelle was swooning over Oscar, the talented older boy who looked just like the poster of the young Baryshnikov in Madame Olenska's office.

6. Alissa had a serious crush on Roberto.

Some of the girls hadn't got such definite opinions yet, and some of them liked three or four boys at the same time, so putting together an accurate list was tricky.

Obviously, the fact that Roberto's name kept coming up worried Zoe a little. She knew she'd never tell him that she liked him, and what could she say even if she were brave enough? Zoe had decided to suffer in silence. She hadn't even told Leda, even though Leda had confessed that she had given her heart to Lucas (although he didn't know anything about it yet).

'Because he's handsome, but he's nice as well,' Leda remarked, as Leda and Zoe sat together at break. 'He's the only really kind boy I know. He never makes fun of anyone and he's always nice when we all play together.'

'When we used to play together, you mean,' Zoe pointed out.

Recently the boys and girls had been spending less time together. The other day when they'd played prisoner ball had been very unusual.

'You're right,' Leda said, after a while. 'Things are different now.'

'If you ask me, we're the ones who are trying to make

things change,' said Zoe, as she and Leda looked out the window.

As usual, the boys were playing football in the play-ground down below. It looked as though the only thought in their heads was winning the game.

'Do you mean that they don't even notice us?' asked Leda, anxiously.

'That's how it seems,' said Zoe, moving away from the window.

The bell rang for the next class. The boys and girls were having separate lessons that day. At least there wouldn't be any awkward boy/girl behaviour in class. It was difficult enough having to deal with Madame Olenska, who seemed to be uncharacteristically light-hearted and bubbly. You could tell by the comments she was making.

'Come on, Alissa, you look like a praying mantis. Relax those elbows. Estelle, your right knee. Do you think you're a frog?' Madame Olenska rapped the floor smartly with her cane.

If they hadn't known better, all the girls would have been laughing, but obviously that wasn't allowed.

When they all moved into the centre of the room to dance, however, the atmosphere suddenly changed, and that little touch of spring that had slipped into the room vanished. There was too much tension and too much concentration.

They were putting together the steps for the most difficult section of the next recital. They'd been divided into groups of three, and each of the groups had to cross the room on a diagonal line, in a sequence of jumps. They weren't difficult as such – Madame Olenska had chosen them carefully to make the girls look really good. The challenge was to synchronise the movements perfectly, so that they all did them at exactly the same time, as dancers in a proper *corps de ballet* should.

Zoe was in a three with Laila and Anna. The method for choosing who went in which group was simple – Madame Olenska divided them up according to height. That meant that Leda had to be in a group with Francine and Alissa.

But Zoe wasn't worried about being in a different group from her friend. She was far too busy concentrating on her feet, her hands, and her body.

Moving in perfect harmony was far harder than the actual jumps, Zoe thought. The piece in question offered the security of a clear, crisp fanfare rhythm, so that it seemed impossible to make a mistake. But it was not enough to follow the music perfectly – the girls had to watch each other in their side vision, attune themselves to each other and keep the right distance between each other. That was complicated, and without awareness a *corps de ballet* could quickly descend into chaos. Zoe, even at this early stage in her training, could spot it when a *corps de ballet* wasn't a top-class one at the professional shows she'd been to. The scenes with the solo dancers might be fine; but the group scenes suffered.

In class everything went surprisingly well. Zoe's group had to repeat the piece only once. Madame Olenska gave the cue to the pianist (in the lessons, dear old Maestro Fantin played a simplified version of the music, but in the theatre, at the actual recital, it would be with a full orchestra) and, the second time, she said, 'That'll do.'

'Good' wasn't a word that Madame Olenska appeared to know. It was strange though, thought Zoe. Madame Olenska had left her homeland such a long time ago that she really should have learned enough new vocabulary by now, and it was such an easy word. But still she never, ever said it.

Zoe stood in the rest position, with her arms relaxed on the barre, and one leg crossed over the other, and watched the other two trios doing their jumps. They did them fairly well, except Estelle, who looked a little pale. She seemed uncertain, which of course Madame Olenska wasn't slow to point out.

Leda, on the other hand, was brilliant, and so were the other two in her group, proving the fact that tall didn't have to mean clumsy. They didn't even need to repeat the exercise again. Suddenly it was the end of the lesson and

Madame Olenska gave the three claps of her hands to dismiss everyone. They were already at the door when she called them back.

'One moment, children.'

I wish she'd stop calling us children, thought Zoe. But she turned round obediently and headed back into the room with the others.

'I wanted to say that the rehearsals are going fairly well. I'm rather happy with you. Even in spite of the springtime, and the sleepiness that's natural at this time of year, you're all paying attention and concentrating. I'm sure that our preparations will proceed as they should. Now you may go.'

They made their way out of the room, one by one, in a stupefied silence. As far as they could remember, it was the first time that Madame Olenska had managed to give them something vaguely resembling praise. Of course, it was meant for all of them, and so it was worth a little less. It would be far more encouraging to receive a compliment just for yourself. But, Zoe thought as she walked back to the changing room, Madame saw them as a class, not as individuals. It was the class that had to be good.

As they were getting changed, they talked non-stop about the strange compliment.

'Maybe she's getting old,' giggled Paula, 'and she's going soft in her old age.'

‘Granny Olenska? Somehow I can’t imagine that,’ said Alissa, pulling a face. ‘I think it was just that she realised we were tired and distracted and she wanted to encourage us.’

‘So you don’t think it was true that we’re *fairly* good then?’ asked Sophie.

‘That’s not what she said. She’s never used the word “good”,’ Paula pointed out, voicing Zoe’s previous thought.

‘Whatever, it was better than when she yells at us,’ said Anna.

‘Yell? Madame Olenska never yells,’ said Paula, very seriously. ‘She just glares at you and that’s all it takes.’

Everyone laughed, and for a moment Zoe felt close to all of the other girls. It would be nice if it were always like that, if they really were allies, accomplices. It wasn’t much to ask really – but the trouble was they each wanted to be the best dancer, and couldn’t help but see the others as rivals.

Zoe was surprised to find Sara’s bedroom door was open when she got home, and, unusually, Sara called out, ‘Zoe, are you home?’ when she walked past.

What stupid things people say just for the sake of it, thought Zoe. *Of course I’m home, you just saw me.* She could be mean and point that out to Sara, who was always the first to make fun of Zoe for any reason. She was tempted to say, 'No, what you just saw was merely a figment of your imagination – I'm still at school.' But instead she stood in the doorway of Sara's bedroom.

'Here I am,' she said. 'How's things?'

Sara's bedroom, just like Maria's, was complete chaos. *What a mess,* thought Zoe, but she didn't say so, because she didn't want to have a pillow chucked at her – or worse.

'Things are totally lame,' said Sara. 'Do you want to listen to some music?'

She pointed at her iPod, which lay abandoned on the bed, the wires of the earphones all twisted up. Sara had *never* lent Zoe her iPod, which was her most treasured possession. *She must have gone crazy,* thought Zoe. She sat down on the edge of the bed and stroked the blue metallic surface of the magic little music box with her index finger.

'No, on second thoughts . . . not now.' Ah, that was more like it. 'Actually, there was something I wanted to tell you,' her sister said. 'I'm in love.'

Not another one, thought Zoe. *It has to be because of the spring.* She felt a little smile twitching on her lips, but she pressed them together and chased it away. Sara would be really annoyed if she laughed. Instead she just looked at her with an interested expression on her face and said, 'Well, go on then.'

'With Stephen,' added Sara, and then she looked away, as if she were embarrassed.

Maybe she really IS embarrassed, thought Zoe, because Stephen was the poor unfortunate who had harboured a crush on her sister since they were four years old and started primary school together. Now they were fourteen, still in the same class and, until today, Sara had never shown the slightest interest in him. How things changed!

'Hey, that's great,' said Zoe. 'I mean, he's been waiting for this for years.'

'And that's the problem,' said Sara, tugging at a lock of hair. 'He's given up waiting.'

'He hasn't got another girlfriend, I hope,' said Zoe.

'No. He's just ignoring me.'

The little smile twitched on Zoe's lips again. Oh, how it twitched! It must be very hard for Stephen to ignore a girl like Sara, with her miles of long blond hair all the way down her back, her blue eyes, long legs and the dimple that made a cute little dent in her right cheek. Difficult? Impossible. It was obviously some sort of plan.

'It's obviously some sort of plan,' Zoe repeated out loud. 'He's suddenly got clever and now he's driving you crazy, the way you've been driving him crazy all these years. I think him ignoring you is just a tactic. He's trying to get his own back on you.'

'You reckon?' Sara suddenly looked hopeful.

How could she not have seen that herself? wondered Zoe. 'I think I'm right,' she said, 'but there's only one way to find out.'

'Let's hear it then,' urged Sara, sitting down and hugging her blue pillow. She looked really good hugging that pillow. *She always manages to do things that make her look good*, thought Zoe.

'Go to him and tell him that you want to be together. You know, that you want him to be your boyfriend.'

'I have to go to him and tell him that I love him?' Sara was stunned.

'I wouldn't say that exactly. Love's a very big word,' said Zoe.

She felt very wise, but she had no idea where this wisdom had suddenly come from.

'But I *do* love him,' said Sara, with a sudden dreaminess.

'Okay, so tell him then. You couldn't be any more convincing,' continued Zoe.

'Shall I go right now? Are my clothes OK? Should I plait my hair? Or wear it down? A bit of make-up? Where's my eyeliner gone?'

That was more like Sara. Zoe smiled inside. Restless, ready to act. And always worried about how she looked.

'You look great as you are. Do you know where he is?' Zoe asked her.

'Of course. Friday afternoon he's always at the practice

sessions down at the basketball court. And if I can't find him, I'll phone him, and if he doesn't answer, that's fine, at least I can —'

'Sara,' Zoe interrupted her. 'You can't send a text message to tell him that you love him. You have to tell him in person.'

'I'm too embarrassed,' said Sara. Her face was hidden behind a curtain of hair as she bent down to do up her trainers.

'So, be embarrassed,' Zoe said. 'But you have to tell him properly. Do it as it should be done.'

Sara was already on the landing when she suddenly turned around and said, 'Don't forget the iPod. I meant what I said before. You can borrow it.'

Then she disappeared. The front door opened and shut with a thud.

Well, that was the closest to a 'Thanks, Zoe' that she'd ever heard from her big sister. She'd have to be content with that. It really had been a pretty exceptional day, Zoe thought, as she picked up the iPod and retreated to her bedroom.

CHAPTER SIX

Gymnastics, Olympic Style

'And one, and two . . . Can you feel it, the music? It's soft. Abandon yourselves to the music. But you must be as exact in your movements as the music is soft. Don't take this as an excuse to become as soft as figs. From the beginning. Let's go. Maestro Fantin, please.'

Soft as figs. It was an interesting expression, and it was not one that Zoe had ever heard before. Perhaps it came from Russia. She tried to behave like a fig, taking advantage of the fact that Madame Olenska was at the other end of the row, paying attention to Francine's shoulders, which, judging from Madame Olenska's comments, had no intention of staying low and straight, as they should. There – legs loose and floppy, hands and arms that seemed determined to touch the ground – that must be how a ripe fig felt. Then Madame Olenska banged her cane, and Zoe understood that she'd better be a very firm fig. Or, even better, a very focused young ballerina.

But, in truth, it was the music that had that effect. Satie's *Gymnopédies* were the piano pieces that would accompany the first part of their recital dance lesson for the recital. Barre exercises were always done with the piano playing in the background, and the *thump thump* of Madame Olenska's cane beating out the rhythm, if the chords weren't clear enough. But this sequence of short pieces was so slow and alluring that you felt like making fluid, languid gestures.

At home that evening, Zoe asked her dad if he happened to have that music by Satie in his CD collection. 'Of course,' he replied, and he played it for her.

At the end of the CD (there were other things on the CD as well and they sat on the sofa side by side, and listened until it had finished), her dad explained to her what he imagined when he listened to the *Gymnopédies*.

'Imagine Greek athletes, from ancient Greece, preparing themselves for a competition, for the Olympics. They're not nervous, not yet. They're doing everything very calmly. They have to stretch their muscles and explain to their bodies that soon they'll have to give their best. Maybe they're rubbing oil on to their skin too. Athletes always used to do that and then they'd compete with each other, their bodies naked and gleaming.'

Zoe tried not to giggle as she imagined the scene.

'But they weren't like us. A naked body was an expression of beauty, not a cause for embarrassment,' her dad added seriously, in response to her smile. 'Think about the most beautiful statues. They're always nudes, male and female.'

Zoe thought about it for a while, as she studied the CD cover with its design of a pear and a green apple. It was a beautiful photograph, but it had nothing to do with Greek athletics, and didn't reflect the music.

Then she said, 'In a way, maybe we're a bit like those athletes too. Because, at the beginning of the lesson, we get ready to do our best and then we perform.'

Her dad nodded silently.

Then he took her hand and said, 'How are you?'

Zoe thought that was a strange question for her dad to ask. After all, she saw him every day, at least in the morning and the evening, and if she wasn't feeling good, he'd notice. But of course it dawned on Zoe that it was a very specific question, and that it had nothing to do with a sore throat or tiredness.

'I'm fine, Dad, honestly,' she said, squeezing her small fingers around his large, strong hand.

'Do you still enjoy what you're doing?'

'Absolutely.'

'A lot?'

'A lot.'

'And it's still more like fun than hard work?'

'Yes.'

'That's fine then.'

It was a strange conversation, Zoe felt. They didn't look into each other's eyes, but sat beside each other, almost as though they were on a train, only they were more comfortable, and more at ease. Zoe knew that her parents worried about her, and that they sometimes thought that their little girl had taken on a burden that was too heavy for her. But ultimately Zoe knew that it was up to her whether to carry on or to give up. She also knew it was up to her whether she became a really good dancer.

No, that's not entirely true, she thought. That didn't only depend only on her – she'd have to see what her body thought about it too. If it would grow in a way that was good for dancing or to become something else – perhaps a body that was perfect for running, or skiing, or playing tennis.

Zoe knew that there were lots of options out there, but

she hoped that things could continue as they were, at least for a bit longer.

In the classroom, during break the next day, Paula was talking about the first part of the recital being a bore, that a comic dance – an entertaining one like the one the third years were doing, for example – would have been better. The third years were performing the *Dance of the Little Mice*. It was true that it was more mime than dance, but at least it was funny, Paula concluded. *Her sister Irene must have shown her the steps at home,* Zoe thought.

'I don't agree,' said Sophie to Paula. 'Come on. Little mice? We're too old to be doing that stuff. In the second year we danced *The Ugly Duckling*. Remember?'

'Of course,' said Laila. Every eye turned to look at her. She never joined in their conversations.

'Oh, you would remember, wouldn't you?' smirked Paula. 'Because you wanted to be the swan at the end, but they asked Leda to do it instead.'

'What's that got to do with anything?' Laila retorted. 'I still had the main part.'

'And I, on the other hand, was the cat . . .' said Paula, and she pretended to stretch, then she miaowed, and then threw herself at Laila in a perfect leap.'The cat that almost ate you all up.'

'Oh, will you stop messing around? You're such little

babies,' Francine said. 'Anyway, I like the dance we're doing.'

'That music sends me to sleep. I bet the audience won't even notice when we've finished our piece. Don't be surprised if no one applauds, they'll all be snoring their heads off,' said Alissa. 'The fanfare section's much better.'

'I think they're both good,' said Zoe. 'First one thing, then the opposite. It feels more complete that way.'

Leda nodded, as she always did when Zoe said something.

'I don't like the fact that we're all doing the same thing,' said Estelle, and this time all of the eyes turned to look at her.

'Just for once, maybe that's nice,' said Leda, boldly.

The girls' eyes moved from one to the other. It was rare for Leda to express an opinion, and in such a decisive way too.

'But we're not all the same,' Laila burst out, and then she bit her bottom lip.

'Thank goodness!' whispered Paula, glancing at Laila, but all of the girls heard her, and they giggled. Zoe couldn't help feeling sorry for Laila once again.

Their history teacher, Mr Langton, was off sick, so after lunch the girls had a free period, or rather, it was supposed to be a study period, but very few of them actually did any work.

Zoe took a piece of paper and started to draw. Zoe wasn't a good artist like Leda, but she did like to play with colours to see how they changed when placed alongside each other. She did what she usually did: she used her ruler to divide the sheet into lots of identical rectangles, then filled each of them in with a different colour – violet next to green which looked bright and cheerful; vivid pink and orange to make you laugh; black and beige to be calming. As she coloured in the rectangles, she thought about what Leda had said.

At one time, they had thought they *were* all the same: right at the beginning, when they were in the first year of school, and had only just passed the entrance exam. With their black leotards still a little on the large side and their brand-new ballet shoes, still in perfect condition, as pink as pale pink can be, they looked like well-behaved little sisters. It had been fun, back then, getting to know each other. Well, most of it had been fun. But some of it hadn't been so great, because, as far as Zoe could remember, Laila had always been as difficult as now.

The least fun thing, however, had been finding out (and it only took a few lessons) that the things they had to do in ballet lessons had nothing to do with ballet – it was all gymnastics. Jump over here! Jump over there! Whirl your arms around! Legs at right angles! Feet flat! Feet flexed! It had been a huge effort getting their young bodies working so hard, and still they didn't even remotely resemble ballerinas.

'You don't get to wear pointe shoes – the ones that help you dance on the tips of your toes – until you're thirteen or even fourteen,' Vicky had explained. She knew a lot of things because her sister Lucy was one of the older girls at the school. 'Before then, you shouldn't even think about it, because they'll ruin your feet. My sister's feet are always bleeding.'

Small as the girls were, they had looked at her with a mixture of fear and suspicion. It seemed impossible that such a gentle thing as ballet could make your feet bleed. Perhaps Ludovica was lying to make herself look more important.

But one day Anna ran into the classroom. 'It's all true. The big girls' feet *do* bleed. I saw one of the girls in the dressing room with bandages wrapped around her foot, all stained with blood, and then she unravelled them and she saw me and tried to hide her foot but I saw it. It was all messy and hurt,' Anna concluded breathlessly.

Demetra, who was not only a costume-maker, but also a bit like a nanny to the girls, had been in the room and reassured them. 'It doesn't happen to everyone. Just girls who have more delicate feet, who find it more difficult to manage the position. That's all.'

Zoe kept on colouring in her rectangles. Red and blue was a contrast so dramatic that it hurt your eyes, she thought, while pink and grey was so gentle.

There was nothing very gentle about dance. There was hard work, and tension, and repetition. The hard work was not always rewarded – sometimes there were steps that you really couldn't manage and your leg seemed determined not to go any higher. Then, suddenly, everything was fine, as if by magic. But it wasn't magic, it was just that you'd been working so hard you'd transformed your body without realising.

Just like preparing yourself for a competition, with the slow, gentle movements of a Greek athlete, Zoe thought to herself, and smiled.

CHAPTER SEVEN

Boys

The invitation was designed on a computer and the colours were a little blocky and faded.

What are you doing on the
afternoon of Saturday 17 April?
You're invited to my birthday party,
at my house, from 4 p.m.
The theme of the party is fancy dress.
Don't forget your costume!
See you there!
Lucas

Zoe was on the phone immediately, ringing Lucas's mobile.

'What present do you want?' she asked him, coming straight to the point.

'Oh, hi, Zoe, how are you? I'm very pleased to hear from you. How kind of you to call,' he teased her.

'Come on, stop messing about and give me an answer. Unless you want things to turn out like last year . . .'

For his birthday the previous year, Lucas received three copies of the same book, two copies of the same game for his Nintendo DS and five football shirts, which had different numbers on, but were all from the same team. To avoid the same mess this year, Zoe thought it would be better to be absolutely clear.

Lucas must have agreed, because he didn't waste time with the usual clichés ('Don't worry about getting me a present, there's no need, really'), that people's parents usually force them to say.

Instead, he shot straight back, 'That DVD we were talking about the other day. It doesn't cost too much and I haven't got it yet.'

Zoe made a note and then asked, 'And what's all this about costumes?'

'Well, I only ever get to dress up at Halloween, so I decided to have a fancy dress party. Don't you think it's a good idea?'

Lucas had a velvety voice, which was unusual for the boys their age. It was low and deep, as if it was growing up faster than Lucas.

Her friends who were in love with Lucas were partly in love with his voice and partly in love with his colour. It was beautiful, a warm, even shade that made his teeth seem whiter and even more twinkling than his dark, dark eyes. Zoe thought he was good-looking, but they'd been friends for so long that she couldn't think about him in any other way.

'Oh, I don't know. I don't really feel like dressing up.'

'Well, just try using a bit of imagination, eh?'

'Is everyone coming?'

'Almost everyone.'

'You don't mean to say you invited Laila, do you?' Zoe asked, and then she immediately felt ashamed of herself, but there was no time to take back the question.

'I've invited her, but she's not going to come,' Lucas said very quickly.

'Did she say that?'

'No, she hasn't said anything. But she never comes to things that we all do together, like the class party or going out for a pizza with the teachers, does she?'

But Lucas was wrong. The party was in full swing and they were bursting the balloons by doing standing jumps on to them (in time with the music, like good ballerinas) when the doorbell rang.

'Who could that be?' said Roberto. 'We're all here . . .'

No. Someone was missing. Laila was missing. And there she was, at the door, shifting the weight of her body from one foot to the other as though desperate for the loo. *No, what a silly idea,* Zoe thought to herself, watching Laila from the back of the room. She just couldn't imagine Laila going to the toilet. She had a present in her hand and she was dressed as a witch, with a spider's web draped over her black pointed hat – clearly an old Halloween outfit.

'Oh, this is for you,' Laila said to Lucas, and she thrust the parcel into his hands.

He gulped and then finally remembered his manners.

'Come in, come in,' he said to her. 'Did you bring a coat? Do you need to take anything off?'

'Yes, she needs to take herself off somewhere else!' Paula laughed out loud.

But the joke wasn't very funny and no one joined in. Zoe had no idea who Paula had come as – she was wearing a short red dress, and had ringlets in her hair.

To release the tension, Zoe did something that she usually did her best to avoid at parties, she jumped on a balloon and made it burst. The bang seemed to get everyone moving again, like the courtiers in *Sleeping*

Beauty when they suddenly awoke from the spell, and the party continued.

'Wonder what she'll do now,' whispered Leda, who'd come as a butterfly and accidentally bopped Zoe on the head with one of her wings.

There were five superheroes, at the party – the best one was Lucas in a Superman outfit. He was also the one who'd made the most effort. It was obvious that the others had borrowed costumes from their brothers or cousins, and Jamie's Batman leggings only reached just below his knees, leaving two very odd knee-length stripy socks on display.

Roberto looked even worse, because no one made pirate outfits for eleven-year-old boys who looked like fourteen-year-old boys, or maybe the clothes sizes in England didn't work the same way for foreign dancers, so it looked as though his top was about to burst open at any moment, creating a rather unlikely Incredible Hulk effect. But they were all having fun, the pizzas were good, the Coca Cola was flowing in rivers, there was sweet *and* salty popcorn (a real treat) and everybody seemed happy.

'Time for the cake!' announced Lucas's mum. It was strange, seeing her beside him, because she was blonde and had green eyes. It was his dad who was black, but he wasn't at home for the party. He was a football player and on Saturdays he was always training or playing in a match.

The cake was really delicious. There were threads of chocolate on the top across a red background that looked as though it might taste of strawberry. The candles were blue, and Lucas blew them out in one go. All twelve of them. In the end, each of them had to fish out their own piece with their fingers, freeing it from the cream and sponge cake beneath.

'And now, let's dance!' cried Lucas.

The music started, and it wasn't Satie or Tchaikovsky or Mozart, none of the stuff that they danced to at school five days out of seven. It was a hard, metallic rhythm that shook their bones and made Zoe feel like she had springs inside. Even Laila left her corner and joined in enthusiastically.

'That dress really suits her,' said Leda, quietly, as she danced next to Zoe.

'Because it's a witch's outfit, you mean?' Zoe asked her.

'Of course. Why else?'

After a lot of dancing and fun, most people began to go home. Soon the only ones left were Roberto, Lucas, Zoe, Leda and Laila. Laila kept looking at the door nervously and kept saying, 'It's strange. Mum said she'd be here at six. Honestly . . .'

Lucas calmed her down. 'You can stay as long as you

want. I'm not going to throw anyone out. And you're not even the last one here.'

Laila looked down at her shoes (long black shoes with buckles – even her shoes were witch's ones) and said quietly, 'It's the first time I've ever been to a party . . .'

'No one would know it,' Zoe said to her. 'You danced the whole time!'

Laila gave a little smile and admitted, 'I like this kind of dancing.' Then she immediately became serious again, as though she'd said too much.

There was no music now. The room was silent. The floor was covered with miles of unravelled streamers and paper chains and party tooters that had been blown so hard that they'd lost their toot and silly little cone-shaped paper hats with shiny stars and spots all over them.

There was that feeling of exhaustion that descends after a party, Zoe thought, when you were happy but dazed at the same time and you wished you were a million miles away, in a quiet, tidy place, calmly thinking back over everything that'd happened. Not very much *had* happened, thought Zoe. It was definitely a good party, though.

The real surprise had been Laila. Zoe didn't know what to think. Maybe Laila's mum had had something to do, so she dumped her at the party? Or was Laila the one who'd asked to come, insisting for the first time after so long? And why? Did she want to make friends with someone? Did she come just because she knew Roberto would be there? Could she still fancy Roberto?

So many questions, and all interrupted by the doorbell. Lucas's mum went to answer it. It was Laila's mum. She had short, boy-like, red hair, and huge hazel eyes, with very long eyelashes. She was tiny, with a ballerina's physique. She looked around the room to find her daughter and her eyes sparkled when she saw her.

'Here I am, darling,' she said, and she opened her arms wide.

Laila dived into the hug, then seemed to remember where she was and let go of her mum, took a step back, and gave an awkward smile.

'Let's just go, Mum.' She turned and waved goodbye, and disappeared. The door shut behind her.

'She's so strange,' said Leda, voicing what everyone else was thinking.

'Who, Laila or her mum? We already knew Laila was strange,' said Lucas.

'You did the right thing inviting her,' said Zoe, and everyone else nodded in agreement.

'I'm pleased she came,' said Lucas. 'It can't be doing her much good being on her own all the time.'

CHAPTER EIGHT

Costumes

'Do you like them?'

Leda had a new pair of jeans, with a low-slung waist and wide bottoms – the kind that trailed behind as you walked, like the train of a princess's dress, except that they actually ended up beneath your shoes all dirty and torn within a couple of days, which was exactly how they were supposed to be.

'Nice,' said Zoe. 'They really suit you.'

And it was true. Her long, slim legs meant that Leda looked great in loose, floppy things that would have looked terrible on a shorter person. These jeans had a small red heart on the right-hand pocket, and a big one in pink and yellow stripes, embroidered on the back of the left leg.

Zoe wasn't very interested in fashion. She liked looking around when she went with her mum and sisters on a clothes raid, as Sara called it, but she preferred the others to give her advice, and, as there were always at least three others (even Maria had fairly strong opinions), she trusted them, and they usually got it right. There was just one thing that Zoe was very clear about, which everyone now knew: she didn't like pink.

'You're a pretty strange ballerina,' Leda had said to her once. 'All ballerinas like pink. Just take a look around.'

They were in the changing room, and Leda was right. What with their wrap-around *cache-coeur* cardigans – the sort that cross over your chest and have woollen ties to keep them closed – and their legwarmers and hair ribbons, it was the usual riot of pink. Zoe narrowed her eyes a little, to make everything go blurred, and the world became full of small, medium and large pink blobs wherever she looked.

Another thing Zoe didn't like was dressing up. Sometimes she thought her fellow students were always dressing up, rather than just getting dressed, without even realising it. They didn't exactly dress in fancy dress, as they had done for Lucas's party, but they *were* still dressing up.

Laila, for example, dressed like a girl from thirty years ago – probably because of her mum. She wore patent-leather shoes (Zoe couldn't remember ever seeing Laila in trainers), pleated kilts, white blouses, red or blue cardigans . . . She looked like the classic good little girl from an old film. All she was missing was a plait or two tied up with bows, and probably the only reason she didn't have those was because school rules didn't allow them.

Alissa, who was the most fashion conscious of the girls (also partly down to her mum), always looked as though she'd stepped out of an advert – one of those silly ones with little girls who wanted to dress like their favourite dolls. As if anyone would ever really want to dress like a doll! Anyway, Alissa absolutely adored really strong colours like fuchsia and bright purple and anything that glittered, and she had these really high shoes with a funny rubber cushion underneath that made her look like a giant and made her walk in a funny way – a bit like a baby goose. She really was quite a sight!

Leda meanwhile was an only child and her mum let her have whatever she wanted. If she asked for something one day, she got it the next. Zoe didn't really approve, but she suspected that she might just be jealous, and so she never said anything about it.

'You should buy yourself something a bit more grown

up to wear,' Leda said to her, with a thoughtful expression on her face.

It was break time, but it was raining, so they were inside. They were in the corridor, looking out of the window at the leaves dripping with water. Sometimes when it rained Zoe felt depressed. When the sun was shining, she never felt sad.

'I think that you must be suffering from meteoropathy,' her mum had told her.

It sounded almost like a disease, or maybe an allergy to shooting stars, but all it actually meant was that her mood changed according to the weather.

'A bit more grown up?' Zoe mumbled, not really paying attention.

There was a little bird in the centre of the yard. It was a tiny thing and it was already soaked through. Why didn't it hop under the tree? The leaves were so thick that the water definitely wouldn't get through them.

'Yes. Something to make you look a bit more grown up,' insisted Leda. 'So that people will notice you.'

'Who? You?' Zoe laughed.

The idea of wearing things so that people would notice her seemed very odd to Zoe. Recently, she'd felt like doing the opposite if anything. She preferred not to attract anyone's attention at all.

'No. You know . . . Roberto, for example.'

Zoe doubted that a colourful T-shirt or a pair of trousers that looked two sizes too big would have any effect on Roberto. She suspected that what would work better on him was her showing an interest in Baryshnikov, football and Playstation.

'Do you really think boys notice how we're dressed? In fact, do you think they even notice us at all?' Zoe asked.

Leda sounded irritated, almost offended. 'My mum says you have to look after yourself if you want people to like you.'

Zoe didn't say anything. She didn't want to argue with Leda. It was raining too much to argue. And anyway she didn't know what to say. Her ideas on the subject were rather confused. It was enough for her to be liked by her family, and Leda, of course, and Lucas. Liked in the sense of enjoying another person's company, being kind to one another, that kind of thing. But she knew that with Roberto, it was another thing entirely. And she also knew that it wasn't something she really wanted to think about right now. Thinking about Roberto gave her butterflies.

It rained all week. Fortunately, there were other distractions. Demetra finally revealed the costumes for the recital, and in their free time there was a constant procession to and from the costume department because everyone liked to look at each other's costumes as well as their own.

The top year were dancing a piece called *Summer*, created for them by Jasper Jones, the director of the Academy Theatre *corps de ballet*. The girls were all going to have wide, stiff tutus in the colours of the sun – yellow, orange, red. The boys were going to be dressed in violet and blue, like streaks of dusk, but of course they had to make do with just a leotard and leggings.

The boys a couple of years above them had wonderful costumes. Their ballet was made up of excerpts from the romantic repertoire, so they had beautiful blue waistcoats like fairytale princes, embroidered in gold, to match the long tutus of the ballerinas.

Lucas and the other boys in Zoe's year were going to wear grey leotards with three-quarter-length sleeves. The girls squealed with joy when they finally saw their tiny tutus in grey and silver – the ones that Zoe had seen the designs for so long ago, but had managed not to tell anyone about. There was also a black tailcoat for Laila, with baggy trousers and braces, a white shirt and a bow tie. *Everything is perfect,* Zoe thought.

All the costumes were hung on a rail, with the name of the student it belonged to attached to each costume with a pin. But there was no costume for Leda, Zoe realised, and she felt her heart lurch.

Leda hadn't noticed, and so Zoe found herself with another secret. It was a much more important one, the sort of secret that itched away so badly that she was desperate to talk to someone else about it in the hopes that the itching would stop. But who could she talk to about it? Not Leda, that was for sure. Zoe was not the one who should have to tell her that she was right to be concerned – Madame Olenska had decided not to allow her to continue and didn't even want her in the recital.

Zoe looked around her. Lucas was busy chatting to Matthew, and she didn't think he'd be very comforting, anyway. There was no one else she thought she could share her worries with.

What made it worse was Leda's concern. 'Are you okay? You look as though you've got stomach ache or something,' she asked Zoe anxiously.

'A bit. I must have eaten something funny,' was all Zoe could manage to say, relieved to have thought of the perfect excuse to go to the toilet for a little breathing space.

In the mirror above the sink, she saw her face was pale. If Leda had to leave the school, her heart would break. And she, Zoe, would be left on her own. She immediately felt ashamed for being so selfish as to worry about herself. What did her own feelings matter when Leda would be absolutely devastated?

Zoe drank a little water from the tap. It was warm and tasted of metal – really disgusting. She dried her hands on a paper towel and rolled the damp shreds of paper between her fingertips nervously. She had decided not to say anything, but she could already feel a knot of anxiety growing in her stomach.

That afternoon, in class, Madame Olenska tapped her cane on the floor three times for their attention.

'I have some news for you. I've made a number of changes to the choreography.'

Here we go, thought Zoe, and she breathed deeply in an effort to slow down her heart, which was thumping away like mad. The others just looked at their teacher with expressions of curiosity on their faces. Leda had also raised her eyebrows with interest. *She obviously doesn't suspect a thing,* Zoe thought.

'You've all been changing recently. That's to be expected as you're growing up. But it has now become clear that not all of you are suited to classical dance.'

You could feel the tension in the air.

'That means that some of you will be unable to do justice to these steps.'

A few nervous feet pawed at the floor. This was it. Who would be out?

'So I have decided to modify part of your ballet. The *Gymnopédies* will remain the same. However, only Alissa and Francine will remain in the last group for the fanfare section. You, Leda . . .'

The moment has come, thought Zoe. She watched the colour drain from Leda's face.

'And you, Lucas . . .'

Lucas? Was he being thrown out as well? But he was really good!

'The two of you will close the performance with a more modern finale, like this. Maestro Fantin, please.'

Maestro Fantin played two thunderous chords on the keys. At the same time, with the dexterity of a conjurer, Madame Olenska threw off her kaftan and turban, and stood there in a black leotard and short, straight black skirt. Her hair was very black, pulled back in a perfect chignon. Everyone was amazed. None of them had ever seen her like this before.

Then Madame Olenska did something else that none of them had ever seen before. She danced to the joyful accompaniment of the music. There was a huge difference between how she was dancing and the graceful and conventional leaps that the groups of three had been performing. She danced just a few steps, then curled her body up, then shot forwards, curled up, shot forwards, then pirouetted on the spot, as fast as a spinning top, before coming to a sudden stop, with arms outstretched. They were beautiful modern ballet steps, not at all like the modern dance Leda detested.

She had finished. Zoe automatically started clapping, before realising that she was the only one. Nobody else dared to join in.

Madame Olenska gave a brief, abrupt bow.

'Those are the steps. Leda and Lucas, you will mirror these movements. And I want you to be perfect.'

That meant that they would have to watch each other as they danced, one facing the other, so that it looked as though one was the reflection of the other. They were so different, but they would have to try to be the same.

'You know that there's not much time left,' added Madame Olenska, 'so we'll start today. I expect you to do additional practice sessions on your own, so as not to disappoint me and your audience. The practice room is also open after school, as you know, until seven in the evening. Get yourselves organised. Now come along, get to your positions. Let's begin. Maestro Fantin, please.'

Zoe leaned against the barre and watched Madame Olenska lead Leda and Lucas along a diagonal line. They did not take their eyes off her and together they imitated her, fitting their movements to the music, letting the notes carry them away. They certainly looked like simple steps, but even the athletic Lucas was hesitant.

Zoe realised now that this was why there wasn't a tutu for Leda on the rail – because Leda would have a leotard and tights identical to Lucas's, in the modern-dance style.

So Leda could still become a real dancer, Zoe thought, *but in a different way. Maybe she could start now, with this recital.*

Leda and Lucas finished their dance, and Zoe watched them running back to their starting point, led by Madame Olenska. Madame Olenska was magnificent, and Zoe never tired of watching her. In comparison, the rest of them were all so clumsy. Well, Madame Olenska wouldn't be dancing in the recital so no one would be comparing them – and by then Zoe knew for certain they'd be so much better anyway.

She looked around the room. All eyes were mesmerised by the scene. Zoe even thought that Laila looked a little envious, but maybe she was just imagining it, probably because that was what she wanted to see. Or maybe Laila's envy was directed at Madame Olenska rather than Leda. It was difficult to imagine that any one of them could ever be as good as her.

But then, they had plenty of time to practise, and you could learn a lot just by watching.

CHAPTER NINE

An Invitation

'What's up, Laila?'

Paula seemed strangely considerate in the changing room as she called over to Laila. She was probably just being nosy. It was Leda who answered, as Laila didn't seem to be able to.

'Hay fever. Terrible, eh?'

And it really was terrible. Poor Laila was slumped in her corner, shaking with a succession of huge sneezes. Her face was blotchy and the skin beneath her nose looked irritated, probably from blowing it too often.

'But that's never happened to her before,' Paula said.

'She said the doctor told her that it can happen suddenly. One year you don't have it, then it kicks off and you have it for the rest of your life,' explained Leda, a little gloomily.

'But isn't there anything she can take for it?'

'Now that she knows she's got an allergy, she can get the medication for it. But she said that the medicine makes her feel sleepy. Either you fall asleep, or you sneeze your head off.'

'Poor thing,' said Paula quietly.

Zoe, who was putting her clothes into her bag, turned around in astonishment. Poor thing? Did Paula really say that? About Laila? How very strange! But this really did seem to be a time for all kinds of weird behaviour.

'She should use proper cloth handkerchiefs, at least they wouldn't rub her skin raw,' said Francine.

'Tell that to her, not everyone else,' Zoe said.

Francine glowered at her, but then she turned towards the corner where Laila was sitting and called out, 'You should use a cloth hanky. Look, I've got one here. Would you like it?'

Between one sneeze and the next, Laila managed to nod, and Francine passed her the precious square of cloth.

'Oh,' Anna cried suddenly, 'my hairnet's torn and it was my last one. Does anyone have a spare?'

Suddenly three new hairnets appeared, still wrapped

in cellophane. Her bun was safe.

Estelle piped up, 'Is anyone going to wear make-up for the recital? Madame Olenska doesn't want us to, but . . .'

'Demetra said she'd do our make-up if we didn't tell everyone,' Zoe replied. 'Just enough to do the job. But we'll have to get in two hours early so that no one sees us.'

As everyone continued to chat, Zoe wondered if this new feeling was what you might call team spirit. In class, everyone continued to think about themselves and their own interests. No one showed any sympathy if anyone was told off. They all just wanted to be as close to perfect as they could, and that meant concentration on themselves.

But apart from Laila, Zoe felt that everyone was full of energy and working hard. But the rehearsals (they weren't having lessons now, just rehearsals) were still very tough, and not without problems. The day before, for example, Madame Olenska been especially critical and when she'd left the room at the end of the lesson they'd all stayed there, paralysed by a fear of failure. What if they were bad on stage? Zoe wondered. Zoe never expressed this worry out loud, but it was certainly shared by everyone else in the class.

Then Laila moved, and it was as though a curse had been lifted from all of them. They left the room slowly, with mechanical movements, like robots that had just been repaired, but which were still rusty.

Zoe was the last one left in the room. Just as she was about to go, Maestro Fantin started to play a very gentle, enchanting piece of music. Zoe realised that it was a waltz, an easy one-two-three, but she didn't know the composer. She stood there in the doorway, without turning around, until the end of the piece.

'Chopin,' Maestro Fantin said then, still hidden behind the piano. 'It breaks your heart, doesn't it?'

'Would you play it for me again?' Zoe said, very quietly, so that he could pretend not to have heard if he wanted.

Maestro Fantin was old and very small, with white hair and round glasses, and he was always smartly dressed, with a jacket, tie and waistcoat. Even when, like now, the weather was starting to get warm.

'Certainly,' he said.

He played two chords, as he always did to indicate that he was about to start. Zoe hardly had time to dash back in to the centre of the room. Then she started to dance.

She'd already done it before, of course, improvising a sequence of steps based on a piece of music that she liked. She danced like that at home now and then. She'd had a Tchaikovsky period; after her mum and dad had taken her to see *The Nutcracker*, the 'Dance of the Sugarplum Fairy' had become almost an obsession. Then there was the Debussy period, although it wasn't easy to dance to that music, which moved as unpredictably as water.

But she'd never improvised at school before, in a proper practice room. She watched herself in the mirror, but it wasn't vanity, it was to check her movements, as proper ballerinas did when studying. And she made a series of solemn steps, slow and a little sad, like the music running over the keys of the piano. At the end she gave the room a deep curtsy.

'Very good,' said Maestro Fantin as she walked past him.

'Were you watching me?' she asked him in amazement. 'Were you playing without looking at the music? Do you know it by heart?'

'Of course. I know all of the music I love by heart,' he answered. 'Have a good afternoon.'

And he stood up, turned away from her and gathered up his musical scores.

There are so many jobs connected to dance, Zoe thought as she left the room. The teachers, the costume-makers, the assistants. And when you did it seriously, there were also lighting technicians and sound technicians, stagehands . . . and down in the orchestra pit, the people who played the music, like Maestro Fantin.

Maybe he really wanted to be a concert pianist up on stage all on his own with a spotlight on him and a breathless audience there for him and him alone. And yet he always played the same music for their lessons – and one and two and three and four. He played for *them*. There were so many people who worked for them. They were so lucky and most of the time they didn't even think about it.

In the corridor, Zoe saw Madame Olenska. 'Excuse me, Madame,' she said, as soon as the thought popped into her head. 'Is Maestro Fantin coming to the recital?'

Madame Olenska looked at her, then stopped in her tracks. 'I don't know,' she answered. 'Maybe he's tired of you. After all, he does see you all every day.'

'Maybe he's not, though,' said Zoe. 'Can we invite him?'

Madame Olenska thought about it for a moment. 'Why not?' she said. 'I can ask Elsa to give him an invitation.'

Elsa was the secretary and getting an invitation out of her was quite a challenge. Each student could have only four tickets, and Zoe gave hers to her parents and sisters. Fortunately, Zoe's gran could use one of Leda's tickets, because Leda had such a small family.

Zoe would have liked to have been able to give an invitation to someone outside her family sometimes – someone like Elisa, the girl who lived a few doors down from them. When they were small they had played together now and then. They couldn't do that any more, because Zoe didn't have much time to play after school, and she imagined that Elisa must have her own things to do as well and her own friends. When they saw each other in the street, they always smiled, and for a moment it was as though they were little again, and Zoe felt free. But that moment vanished so quickly. And maybe Elisa wasn't interested in dance anyway.

Zoe was delighted when Ms Elsa said she would give Maestro Fantin an invitation. She hoped he would come – and Zoe was sure he would.

CHAPTER TEN

The Dress Rehearsal

The moment of truth had arrived. They say that if the dress rehearsal goes badly, the actual performance will be perfect, and the other way round, so Zoe never knew whether she wanted the rehearsal to go well or not as obviously she wanted the performance to be perfect. Messing it up on purpose didn't count, and nobody would do that and risk humiliation in front of the entire school anyway. Zoe hoped that if that happened, the ground would open and swallow her up, or a trapdoor would open in the stage beneath her feet, so she could slip away. Or maybe melt away like a snowman, leaving behind just a soggy puddle to be quickly absorbed by the wood of the stage.

It was wonderful to have a proper dressing room instead of the usual changing room. There was a big mirror with lights all around for doing make-up, but all it reflected to Zoe were her own defects. Zoe looked at herself and thought that her mouth was too big, and there was nothing she could do about that, even with make-up. Actually, she felt like rubbing her lips together to get rid of the touch of lip-gloss that Demetra had allowed everyone to have – it seemed to make her lips stick out even more than usual.

'What are you doing? If you do that, you'll rub your lip-gloss off, and there's still an hour to go!' Leda shrieked at her.

Zoe shrugged her shoulders and turned her back on her reflection.

'That's right. Be a nice girl and get out of the way so I can take a look at myself in the mirror,' said Anna, nudging in beside her.

Zoe did as she was told and sat down on one of the chairs placed around the walls of the dressing room. She should have felt full of energy, but all of the waiting had worn her out.

If Madame Olenska was surprised to see them all ready so far in advance, she didn't say anything. She was too busy with the little ones, who, as usual, were in complete chaos.

Zoe walked past their dressing room. The door was open and she saw one of them crying her eyes out. Three of her friends were trying to console her, but they were having little success, and it looked as though they were all about to burst into tears themselves.

Zoe leaned against the doorframe and said, 'You all look so lovely.'

They really did, in their little black leotards, with headdresses of white roses. The girl who was crying had knocked her headdress so it was lopsided. Zoe tidied it up for her and stroked her hair. Then, using a tissue on the table, she dried her tears.

'I bet you're going to be really good,' she said. The girls all seemed transfixed by her now.

When Zoe peeped at herself in the mirror, surrounded by all of those little round faces, she realised that to them she really did look wonderful. Those silver threads in the tulle of her tutu and in her hair looked very impressive.

'Bye then, girls,' she said. 'See you on stage. I'll keep my fingers crossed for you.'

And she left, feeling grown up – really grown up.

Then, in the corridor, Zoe walked past eight sylphs in long, white tutus and pointe shoes and she suddenly felt small again – really small! She even pressed herself against the wall to allow them to pass, not daring to brush against the soft tulle of their rustling skirts.

'It's going to be really good,' one of the sylphs said to her friends.

She gave Zoe a movie-star style smile over her shoulder, framed with real red lipstick. If she said so, thought Zoe, it must be true.

Zoe went back to the dressing room, and noticed Laila was silent and her eyes were lowered.

'She took a pill for her hay fever, because she couldn't stand it anymore,' Francine explained sympathetically. 'So she's just having a nap.'

Laila's eyes flashed upwards, but her voice was soft, almost polite. 'I'm not sleeping,' she said. 'I'm just resting my eyes.'

They all laughed, but it wasn't mean laughter, it was gentle and understanding.

'Tell you what,' said Francine. 'We'll let you know when it's quarter of an hour until the rehearsal, so that you can do some *pliés* to wake yourself up. To warm yourself up, I mean.'

Laila nodded, but said nothing. A strange silence descended upon the dressing room. Usually they would all be chattering away.

Zoe looked at her classmates. The make-up had made all of their complexions look similar, but you could still clearly see how pale Leda was. Alissa, on the other hand, was a bit flushed, as though she had a bit of a temperature.

That always happened to her when she got excited.

'Anyone need a touch more lip-gloss?' Anna dared them, and she took a silver container out of the pocket of her jacket, which was hanging on the coat rack.

'You know, we've already gone too far with this. If Madame Olenska notices, she'll be really angry,' said Sophie, nervously.

'Of course she won't notice! With all that she's got on her mind? And anyway, if we're all wearing it, and our mouths look the same, she'll never be able to tell. Come on, who's first?'

And with the cool self-confidence of an experienced make-up artist she opened the tube, pushed up the shiny liquid, took a tissue from the box on the table and gave the top a good clean.

'Me next!' Paula stepped forward.

She sat down in front of Anna, who remained standing and concentrated on her work. Everyone put on more lip-gloss, aprt from Laila of course, who was dressed as a man and even had a moustache drawn above her top lip.

Now they really were all ready, and they crowded around the magnificent mirror to admire themselves. It looked like a photograph, thought Zoe, one of those photographs that you saw in magazine articles about the most famous dance schools in the world of which their school was one. You always saw those smiles accentuated by the red gleam of the lipstick, that hair pulled back really tight, those starry eyes.

It suddenly seemed as if the hard slog, the rivalries and dissappointments and jealousies were all forgotten when it came to the actual recital. As they all smiled happily in front of the mirror, waiting to show everybody what good ballerinas they could be, Zoe realised that all the effort involved had been worthwhile.

And then the moment was gone. Clarice, the stagehand, opened the door without knocking.

'It's almost time. Everyone on stage! Let's hope the boys are ready too,' she said and left.

Laila didn't have time to warm up, but it didn't matter as she suddenly seemed to be wide awake and watchful, her eyes darting about, distant, almost devoid of expression.

Zoe pressed up close to Leda, who whispered to her, 'Are you nervous?'

No, Zoe wasn't scared. It was the dress rehearsal. And she wouldn't be nervous even in three days' time because she found the excitement chased the fear away, and it fled before the magnificent prospect of the stage (a real stage, the stage of the Academy Theatre) with its vast space which they had to conquer.

The door to the stage was painted black and marked with a red light. When the light was on, you couldn't go in. Now the light was turned off. Clarice opened the door, whispering, 'Come on through.'

On the other side, everything was black – all the walls and the hanging cloths that made up the wings. When she saw them for the first time, years ago, Zoe had found herself following their entire length with her eyes, up, up, all the way to the tangles of pipes and scaffolding that make up the ceiling of a theatre, and she'd felt almost dizzy. Then she got used to it and learned to pick out her spot and stand in the right position, so that from the other side, from the stalls, no one could see the ballerinas preparing for their entrance.

Caroline, the other stage assistant, called them over silently, waving her hands and mouthing, 'Over here.'

They had to be quiet, but that was quite easy with their soft shoes. The older girls who were wearing pointe shoes, had to tread gently so that they didn't create a hail of thuds. The third and fourth years were on stage together now, a kind of friendly zoo that included mice and cats. They were bouncing all over the place like little rubber balls and Madame Olenska was shouting, above the music, 'Strawberries! Strawberries!'

No, she hadn't gone mad. The strawberries were the fluorescent stickers that had been stuck to the stage to show clearly where every cat and every mouse had to stand. When they were bouncing around like mad, it was tricky to land in the right place every time, and some of them were making a real mess of it. But at the third cry of 'Strawberries!' they all returned to their places.

There, they'd finished, the mice on one side, the cats on the other and the stage wings ready to swallow them up. The curtain beside Zoe twitched and was pushed aside as a gang of felines rushed by. It flapped against Zoe's cheek for a moment. Zoe loved the smell of cloth and dust.

And now it was their turn. As the first four chords of *Gymnopédies* rang out, the boys entered from the other side of the stage. They each went to their positions (they had apples, not strawberries). The first in line was Estelle, the smallest one. The last one, of course, was Leda.

'Quickly, girls, you're on!' whispered Caroline, giving Estelle a push.

From the wings, Zoe could see the large black well of the stalls and the brilliant strip of spotlights surrounding the stage, nothing else. The music started – it was their music, her music. Now they just had to follow it, let themselves be carried along by it and everything would go as it should go: brilliantly.

CHAPTER ELEVEN

Finale

Not only did the dress rehearsal go well, but the actual performance was a success too. Laila didn't fall asleep, Leda and Lucas received a round of applause all for themselves, and the grand finale was, as always, magnificent. The whole school lined up on stage, row by row, year by year, the lights went on and the applause multiplied as the crowd went wild, shouting and smiling, so that every dancer felt part of something big, something special.

After the curtain dropped, a strange calm fell upon the dancers as well. There was no rush of chatter to break the stillness. Even the busiest tongues seemed to be still.

They found Maestro Fantin waiting for them as they returned to the dressing room. He was holding a bouquet of little pink roses, and as the girls passed, he gave each one a brief smile then handed them a rose.

Zoe was the last one to arrive.

'Oh, look,' he said. 'I've still got three roses left. I imagine they must all be for you then.'

She smiled as she took them and gave him a deep curtsy. He responded with a nod of his head.

As they were getting changed in a confusion of leotards and tights and shoes and T-shirts, there was a knock at the door.

'Come in,' Laila said, answering for all of them.

It was Madame Olenska.

'I am satisfied,' she said, passing her gaze over each of them, one by one. 'You all behaved very well.' And then she added, 'I'll see you in class on Monday. Revision of the barre exercises for the examination.'

When she closed the door, Anna mimicked her, 'Revision of the barre exercises for the examination,' she said, with her nose in the air and her eyes half closed.

'I think it was her way of saying that we were good,' Zoe said. 'She's never said anything like that before. At the end of the other recitals, I mean.'

'You're right,' Laila said, and she gave an incredibly

loud sneeze that made the room shake. The pill must have stopped working.

They all burst out laughing.

Zoe was the last one to leave: she liked to take her time.

'I'll wait for you outside,' Leda said.

Zoe nodded, putting on her trainers. She now had the mirror all to herself and she looked in it one more time. She was surprised to see that her make-up hadn't worn off. The touch of pearly grey eye-shadow made her eyes look a bit bigger and her mouth was still a little too red. Above the blue T-shirt and the jeans, her face no longer looked like her own – it looked out of place. So she took a make-up removing tissue from her bag (a present from Sara, who had a whole pack of them and used them every night before bed) and she wiped it all over her face. When she'd finished, her skin was fresh and a little damp and there was a slight scent of roses in the air.

Roses. Zoe put her bag over her shoulder and, last of all, picked up Maestro Fantin's three roses from the table. Looking back over her shoulder as she left the room, she realised that some of her classmates had forgotten their roses in their hurry, so she added them to hers, and her bouquet grew larger.

Outside, the sun was still shining (after all, it was only six in the evening and nearly summer) and patches of sunlight were filtering cheerfully through the leaves of the tall trees. Some of the others were still waiting outside. Lucas waved her over.

'We're all going to go for a pizza, but we're going to the park for a while first,' Lucas said.

When Zoe got home, she was exhausted, but she made sure she arranged the six little roses in a white vase on her bedside table.

Having roses near and all to herself seemed very grown up and feminine, Zoe thought as she lay in bed that night. One of the roses had started to shed its petals – two petals had fallen on to the glass top of the bedside table. They were beautiful too.

Zoe looked at them; they almost gleamed in the dark. It wasn't absolutely pitch black in her room. She never completely closed the blinds, so the light from the street was enough to illuminate her roses, so bright and radiant.

Zoe felt so happy. It had been an evening of hugs and congratulations as everyone said it was the best show they had seen.

The school year wasn't over yet – there were still the exams to come. In the world of dance, there would always be another obstacle to tackle; another test to face; another goal to achieve. Zoe smiled. She was moving forwards, towards the future, ready to dance.

Ballet Academy

Ballet Academy

A Question of Character

BEATRICE MASINI

Zoe is glad to be back at Ballet Academy after the summer holidays and can't wait to begin their character dance lessons – classes full of fast steps and excitement.

Life outside of school seems just as eventful – Zoe's friendship with Leda is turning frosty and she's not sure why, but Roberto is being more friendly than usual! It's up to Zoe to figure out what it all means, and make sure her dreams stay on track!

Sheridan Winn

THE CIRCLE OF POWER

'I've got a magic trick!'
said Ariel. 'Watch!'
She pointed her finger at Flame's purple bra.
It lifted off the chair and hovered in the air.
Marina and Ash laughed.

Each of the Sprite Sisters, aged between nine and thirteen, has a magical power related to one of the four elements – Earth, Water, Fire or Air. When Ariel discovers her power on her ninth birthday, their circle is complete. The girls' magic must be kept secret, and used only for good; if not, the consequences could be dire.

The Sprites' big house in the country is full of laughter and sunshine, but a shadow is falling. Everything the Sprite Sisters hold dear will soon be shattered by the arrival of someone who is intent on destroying their power . . .

Girl Writer

Ros Asquith

Cordelia Arbuthnott wants to write books. Not the sort that her aunt, the bestselling children's author Laura Hunt writes, but literary masterpieces.

So when she finds out that her dreaded new school Falmer North is having a writing competition, she's delighted. She just knows her medieval love story, *The Lady of the Rings*, will win the romance category.

But writing a masterpiece is trickier than she expected. What with wanting to make a good impression at Falmer North, sorting out her best friend Callum's home problems, and coping with her eccentric family, real life just keeps getting in the way.

Featuring fantastic top tips on getting your story right.

THE ISLAND THAT WASN'T THERE

Ruth Snowden

His one eye was green, like the smooth glass pebbles you find on the shore. It stared at us without blinking. And his empty socket seemed to stare too, like there was a hidden eye in it.
I screamed. I didn't mean to – it just burst out with the shock of it.

Rosie and her friends are fascinated and terrified by Yan Eye – an old man who's a stranger to their town and barely says a word. But when Rosie needs help, Yan Eye is the only one who will believe her.

She finds herself in a boat with him, rowing towards an island that wasn't there before – and it's soon down to Rosie to make unlikely new friends and break the curse gripping the strange island of Hildaland.

A mysterious, beautifully told story by a wonderful new author.